About the author

Peter Hanrahan is sixty seven and married to Linda (45 years). They have been blessed with six children, eleven grandchildren and four wonderful son/daughters in-law. Formerly working in education as a teacher and headteacher, he is now 'retired', though having retrained as a teacher of English, he teaches English as a foreign language whenever he gets the opportunity, preferably somewhere hot and sunny, or Budapest. He writes to escape crowds, see above, and has been meaning to complete this sequel to the original 'Croissant', for ages. Finally, having rented a cottage in Brittany, in January 2022, he locked himself away and did it! This masterpiece therefore was written in France, proofed in Budapest and hopefully, read all over the world!

I hope that these tales of travelling make ya smile.

Peter

~~Croissant~~ Crossing the Channel

Next Stop, France

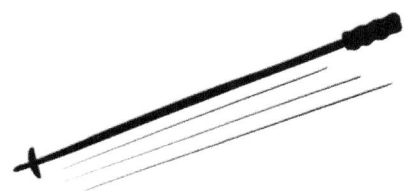

BY

Peter Hanrahan

Abbey Lakes
Books

Copyright © 2022 Peter Hanrahan

All rights reserved

The characters and events portrayed in this book are fictitious. Any similarity to real persons, living or dead, is coincidental and not intended by the author.

No part of this book may be reproduced, or stored in a retrieval system, or transmitted in any form or by any means, electronic, mechanical, photocopying, recording, or otherwise, without express written permission of the publisher.

ISBN: 9798839508170

Cover design by: Art Painter
Library of Congress Control Number: 2018675309
Printed in the United States of America

Many thanks to Joe for the brilliant cover. Pam for her patience in proofing and also Christie and Judith for their contribution too. For all the family who energise me and most of all Linda who for forty-five years plus, has kept me on the straight and narrow, poured oil on troubled waters, papered over the cracks, managed my ventures, and generally enabled things to happen.

CHAPTER 1

"Skiing!?!!"

Denis, now approaching his very late 50's, moaned plaintively in response to his son Jack.

"But I haven't done it for over thirty years. Last time I was, well, younger and fitter, and more importantly, bounced when dropped. Things don't work like they used to anymore Jack. I've got a back and two knees, an ankle and two thumbs, and one of me hips is beginning to make noises too!"

Denis had not coped well with the inevitable encroachment of the autumn of his life. In fact, he hadn't coped at all. He had for instance, well at least since turning thirty, struggled with his inability to retain a healthy weight. It seemed that having been a constant ten stone (in old money), from shortly after birth, he had, since reaching the significant milestone, begun to display the first signs of approaching middle age. At first he was, without actually voicing it, in a kind of denial, whilst dismissing any thoughts of weight gain he pretended to himself that his clothes were just mysteriously getting smaller,

"Anyhow," he would delusionally console himself, "That top button was always a bugger to fasten."

It was when even his trousers had mischievously joined in, that shivers of alarm had begun to literally ripple through his extra pounds and he began to fear the worst.

Eventually, as is often the case, it was the unexpected glimpse of a photograph, when the proverbial penny had dropped. His immediate reaction had been;

"Who's that fat git?" Followed almost immediately with;

"Oh, it's me!"

Recovering from the initial shock, he resolved that action was indeed necessary.

Unfortunately, as is the inevitable consequence of getting older, the arrival of the unwelcome weight gain proved only to be the scouting party. Having become something of a permanent feature for Denis, it was quickly followed by the other signs, the things not working properly anymore. From back, to ankles, to knees and latterly even the thumbs!

"What 's that all about?" moaned Denis,

"I've hardly used the bloody things!"

The final humiliation was the realisation that his hair was no longer fitting as well as it used to either!! This particular shock had also been delivered rather cruelly, courtesy of the unexpected sight of the back of his head, in the ceiling mirror of a local DIY store.

Denis however, was not alone in his struggle to deal with the unfortunate consequence of being as it were, 'born astride the grave'. Always at his side was his far more prosaic and practical wife Maisie. Hailing from either side of the Pennines, in the North of England, Denis and Maisie Wilson were quite different in their outlooks. Though happily, most of the time these differences, rather than causing any friction, actually complimented each other.

Ever so slightly younger than Denis, Maisie his companion of ages, had been brought up in the down-to-earth surroundings of a farm, in a family that had been farming since shortly after the invasion of William the Conqueror. She was therefore, far more in tune with the cycles of life and the patterns of growth, development, and yes getting old, and happily far more at ease with her own changing profile. Just like the little brook running through the farm of her childhood, she had learnt to go with the flow of life and if any obstacles came her way she just pushed through them or if necessary skirted round. She certainly never stopped and dwelt. Her counsel for her husband was as simple as it was sensible,

"Just get some bigger trousers Denis!"

This unwelcome advice, had to some extent, kicked Denis into gear, and as a result of various strategies and slimming regimes, he had eventually successfully managed to fit better into his size 36s. Sadly for Denis, as farmer Maisie had also helpfully pointed out, in a similar way to pruning a hedge, cutting weight served only to encourage further growth, so the benefits were frustratingly temporary. Despite this, and contrary to his dear wife's advice, Denis refused to give in to the inevitable and stubbornly refused to buy bigger trousers. Encouraged by his son Jack, he desperately clung onto his vigour.

Despite his initial protestations and the reality check of his advancing years, Denis's vanity had conquered his reason and Jack had convinced his Dad that skiing together in the Pyrènees would be "Awesome!!" and that everything would be "Cool."

So, sometime after the latest unpleasant discovery regarding his stage in life, here he is perched high up in the mountains in France, on the top of a 'red' ski slope, and looking down what appears to be a sheer drop. In the distance, viewed hazily through the powder spray left behind by extremely competent skiers, are some rectangular dots, representing chalets, and other outlets associated with the resort far below.

"Oh God help me!" he quietly implored.

"Jack, I did tell you that your father is not as young as he used to be. Certain bits don't work as well anymore and some, like shock absorbers and suspension, not even at all."

It seemed that by rehearsing again the reasons why he shouldn't be two thousand metres up on the edge of a red run in the snowy Pyrènees, it might make it all disappear and he would be back down, gliding along sensibly on some nice meandering 'green' slope. Neither was his agonising tempered by the encouraging words of his dear practical wife Maisie that were constantly ringing in his ears,

"Skiing! At your age Denis, really?"

Jack, the youngest offspring of Denis and Maisie Wilson, had inherited his father's love for La Belle France to the extent that, having met and married Symone whilst on a lager-fuelled stag weekend in Morlaix, (well not married her the same weekend of course) was now living and working close to the mountains of Southern France. Sharing his leisure time between body boarding and snowboarding, depending on the season, he had, just that morning, been reassuring his father that what he had learnt to do all those years ago would, like riding a bike, soon come flooding back.

Due to his dad's passion for all things French, Jack, along with his sister Clare, had spent most of his childhood holidays soaking up the experiences on offer in various areas of the country. When given the opportunity to live and work in Pau with its snow-capped mountains and Atlantic beaches just a short drive away, it hadn't taken Jack much time to sign on the dotted line. Symone was equally enthusiastic and happy to move south to the sun. Her parents, Breton farmers, who had never really got over Agincourt et al. were not so enamoured with their only daughter being kidnapped by some English Knight but when they learnt that he was vaguely from farming stock they had relented and even on occasion made the journey down to the mysterious south for a visit, and a look at the famous Limousin cattle on the way. It was also an opportunity to enjoy a bit of the South of France sunshine. Morlaix's weather, could like an English summer, be equally capricious.

Jack was well and truly settled in his newly adopted country; plenty of sunshine, trips to Spain, snow and sea. The 'little fellah' had grown into a strapping young man and now towered over his father and mother. His older sister Clare, who used to love him and hate him in equal measure was a regular visitor with a series of boyfriends but never the 'right one'. She often found herself babysitting the newly arrived Florence.

"Some things never change." reflected Clare, who used to have to chaperone Florence's dad all those years before and time had done little to temper her sense of the unjust.

It was the arrival of Florence Eva Denise Wilson, that had prompted this latest English invasion. Accompanying the Wilsons were their old travelling companions Eddie and Gloria Lancaster. Eddie, with bad knees and Gloria, with not enough sense of balance to master a bicycle let alone skis, had decided that being holed up in a warm house in the company of several bottles of sweet, white, 'Jurancon' wine, seemed the better option. Maisie, who rarely succeeded in dissuading Denis from his little escapades, though not through want of trying, was also back at the ranch waiting for the inevitable phone call….

"Did dad bring his European Medical Card with him?"

"God forbid." she thought, sinking her third glass of Kia Royale.

Eddie, from South London, had skied before when he was in the Territorial Army but it was cross-country skiing and he did have bad knees. He had in fact reprised his skills on the dry ski slope in Plymouth anticipating joining Denis and Jack for the real thing but, after tripping over on his first descent, he gracefully declined the opportunity to 'powder the Pyrènees'. The fact that he clearly hadn't been downhill before hadn't helped and so along with Gloria's encouraging words;

"Eddie you are not going skiing!" still smarting in his ears, his decision had been made.

The scorch marks on his backside from his long journey to the bottom of what was effectively a giant toothbrush, kind of sealed it too. However, his 'bad knees', did enable him to retain his honour, but he did get a little bit irritating with his,

"If I didn't have this 'pair-a-nees', oid be with you in the Pyrènees!" Yes, thank you Eddie.

A few weeks earlier and sitting in the safe and comfortable surroundings of a pub, Denis had declared with authority to his wife and friends.

"You never forget a skill that you learnt in your youth. That's what I believe."

But the conviction in his voice slowly began to wane in concert with his wife's slowly ascending eyebrows.

"Yeh. He learnt to do handsprings and somersaults in his teens but he doesn't seem to do them any more Glo." retorted Maisie.

Eddie looked at the floor, hiding his grin, Gloria didn't bother, she just laughed out loud.

"Denis, last time you skied." continued Maisie sensing the upper hand.

"Clare was waking-up every four hours and Jack was still in heaven. You hadn't even heard of sciatica or arthritis of the thumbs. And you had a full head of hair!"

"Ouch, that last one was a bit cruel." thought Eddie who tried to pitch in.

"Oh, come on Maisie."

"Shut up Eddie." flashed Gloria, which he did. "Don't you get any ideas."

After a long pause, Denis said rather randomly,

"Anyway, I learnt to play the piano when I was in my youth."

"Oh, I give up Denis, do your own bloody thing. But don't scream for me when you're in the rescue helicopter."

"Result!!" thought Denis. "Maisie's blessing."

He was confident that if things did go a bit awry, she would be there to pick up the pieces. Well not literally of course.

"Another pint Eddie?"

Now on this chilly but beautifully sunny February morning, after the initial trepidation at the thought of hitting the piste again after all those years, Denis's long-anticipated return to the ski slopes had started rather well.

Everything had been going very well in fact. Denis had managed to get his boots on, no mean feat, and had even managed to get himself onto the nursery slope where though he had been lapped several times by some little 'smart-arse' French toddlers, he wasn't discouraged. He was still standing after all, having only wiped out on two occasions and one of those was when he had collided with one of the 'bloody toddlers'.

His hips were beginning to swing, his feet were beginning to stop burning and his confidence was reaching dangerous levels of delusion. Whilst soaring in these dizzy heights of self-confidence and convinced that his earlier reference to, 'never forgetting a skill', had indeed been prescient, he allowed Jack to convince him that his period of probation on the nursery slopes was well and truly over and he was ready to laugh in the face of blue runs and red runs and who knows what!

But now, just a short time later and peering over the edge, all he could think of was, 'scream,' 'rescue' and 'helicopter.'

"Oh Lord." he thought. "What if I fall and my ski bindings don't release my boots? What if I can't stop. It's miles to the bottom. What if I go off through those tapes at the edge of the run and fall off the bloody piste altogether and into a huge snow drift! Jack! I told you!!"

And that's when it started to snow again

"I hope that they are alright." said Maisie. "It's a long time since Denis skied."

"I'm sure that Jack will look after him Maisie." responded Gloria, not really listening.

"It's just that the last time he went skiing, me and him were going up on one of those 'T' bars, and when he slid off at the top, his side of it slipped up his ski jacket and started dragging him up towards the big wheel at the top of the run. I could only scream and scream until this nice handsome young man shot down and turned the machine off. That was thirty years ago when he was young. I can see it now as if it were yesterday, it was awful. Oh God, he could have been killed!!!"

"Calm down Maisie, calm down. He'll be fine. I didn't know that you had been skiing. Another Kia?"

"Yeh, go on then. Why not?"

The day had started perfectly. Jack had managed to supply all of the extra gear which Denis remarked dismissively, wasn't around in his day. Thermal vest, proper ski socks, long johns, goggles! Symone had packed them enough food to keep them going for several days and Denis had brought some Kendal Mint Cake he'd found in the drawer at home.

"Just in case eh Jack, ha ha."

"It's pouring down with rain you know Denis?" Maisie had pointed out as they were setting off.

"Don't worry that's fine, it'll be falling as snow up the mountain." Jack replied reassuringly.

"Yes, but it's *pouring!!*" she added. "That's the point. And it's windy"

"Why did Maisie always need to be so smart." thought Denis.

(Probably being married to you Denis.)

By the time they reached the climb up to the ski resort of Ax Les Thermes, the rain was indeed falling heavily and by the time they were close to the pretty little spa town of the same name, still several miles from the ski village, it had turned to snow. Heavy snow.

"I think we may need to stop in the town and get some chains." suggested Jack. "It's not usually this bad on the road and we have a way to go yet."

The sight of a huge coach that had skidded halfway into a ditch confirmed this.

Finding snow chains in a village full of enterprising French vendors was not a problem, even the boucherie stocked them! But having to wait until the vendors had finished their mandatory two-hour lunch break was more frustrating.

"I was hoping to get skiing by one at the latest." Jack moaned.

But by the time they had fitted the chains, no easy task, and completed the distance, it was nearer three in the afternoon. Denis had been charmed by the journey through the winter wonderland, Jack was less impressed, especially as one of his wipers wasn't working and he knew just how close the edge of the road was. Denis, oblivious, was entranced, and every so often dutifully leaned out of the window to clear the snow off the windscreen so that Jack could see. Eventually, they arrived at the busy resort and put the journey behind them.

Denis had forgotten just how difficult it was to walk in ski boots and hadn't the faintest as to what size his feet were in France, never mind his weight in kilogrammes, but the guys in the rental shop were well used to helping the old and infirm and soon sorted him out. The only time that Jack had felt the need to intervene was when his dad was asked his level of competence. Denis managed only,

"Well, when…"

"Débutante." interrupted Jack

"Short skis, 160's Monsieur?"

"Er oui. Er merci." said a sheepish Denis.

After a few goes on the nursery slope, Denis did indeed feel it all come 'flooding back', and he was soon ready for 'les bleus'. Unfortunately, the snow by now was well and truly falling blizzard style. This is the excuse, Jack later and forever after, used to explain to his mother why he had mistakenly led his father, who was skiing for the first time in thirty years, onto the wrong cable lift and he had ended up perched precariously on the precipice of a true red.

By the time they had reached the summit of the gentle 'blue', the snow had ceased and the view over the surrounding peaks was magnificent. As he slipped off the chairlift and wheeled confidently to the right towards the start of the piste his comment to Jack should have started the alarm bells tinkling at least a little, it did with his son.

"Blimey it took nearly half an hour on that chair lift. We'd better get down quickly or we won't get too many goes. What magnificent views. Isn't it amazing we seem to be looking down on all the other peaks."

And that's when the snow came back.

"What time did you say the boys were due back Maisie?" enquired Gloria, conscious that the 'antipasta' as described by Symone had been consumed nearly five hours ago and she hadn't even seen any of the pasta.

"Oh, six-thirty, sevenish, I think. They're bringing some entrecôte back with them."

"Oh wow?" said Gloria.

"Steak." whispered Eddie helpfully.

"Any time soon then, thank goodness for that."

So, this really was the moment of truth.

"Go on dad, you'll be fine, just take it slowly."

"Oh yeh." thought Denis, "take it slowly, just like if you fell out of an aeroplane."

He did consider the options, but other than taking off his skis and trying to find his way two thousand metres down a mountain in great big boots and a blizzard. There really weren't any. The only choice was right before him.

"I don't believe this." was his final thought before saying his "Oh Jesus!" prayer and going for it.

Denis made it about fifteen metres before wiping out. By the time he tried to turn to control his descent his speed was such that he couldn't, and down he went in a tangle of skis and poles. That's my knee gone he managed to surmise through the agony. He lay in a heap, a cold sweat beginning to creep over his crumpled body. Denis whose life was generally represented by the half-full glass rather than the half-empty one was suddenly enveloped by what could only be described as a mid-life crisis. Why oh why had he ignored Maisie's words of wisdom?

"Skiing? At your age Denis?"

As he lay there wallowing in a heap of self-pity with the developing blizzard limiting his world to the immediate location, he convinced himself that he was about to die.

"Just imagine that." he thought to himself. "So, this is how it ends, Maisie will be livid. Just as well I am on the way out really." And then chuckled as he considered the illogical thought.

As the swishing sounds of fellow skiers went rushing past his broken frame, Denis's thoughts were rushing through his mind. Like some jealous suitor, the country with which Denis had been in love since his first foray all those years ago as an eighteen-year-old, was now refusing to allow him to leave.

"How ironic," he thought, "how poetic, how French………."

Denis resigned to his fate and settling back into the embrace of the surrounding snow, felt a sense of calm. As he peacefully drifted off into the inevitable, precious recollections of times spent in La Belle France, like a funeral cortège, began accompanying him on his final journey.

As his mind wandered through the wonderful memories of many previous adventures in France, ever positive Denis comforted himself with one thought…

"What a way to go!"

At least they would find him with a smile on his face…….

CHAPTER 2

Promenading along the magnificence of the Cannes harbour side on the French Riviera, Eddie was feeling a little discouraged at his wife's response to his suggestion.

"Nah, Eddie, I'm not sure I fancy it." said Gloria, "All day in a boat! What if it gets rough? Anyway, you get sea-sickness Eddie, it'll be a bit of a waste of money if you spend the day throwing up again like you did last time we went on the ferry to Roscoff."

"It's not just sailing around in a boat, and anyway that was an extraordinarily rough crossing." Eddie replied defensively.

Denis, listening attentively to his friend's attempt to convince his 'land-locked' wife of the attractions of spending a day on a boat (good luck with that one Eddie), smiled to himself as he remembered that particular episode. It had been the kind of storm which had convinced the travellers as they approached the Plymouth docks, that their Brittanty Ferries trip across the Channel would be abandoned, or at least postponed by 24 hours, but they had not accounted for Capitaine Jules's,

 "Ze show must go on." approach to seamanship.

Despite the apocalyptic nature of the October storm, the procedure for boarding was very much business as usual. Apart from that is being greeted at the cavernous mouth of the ferry boat by a huge phalanx of French stevedores ready to shout,

"ALLEZ!!"

This noisy greeting was aimed at the car drivers. It was a command carefully timed to coincide with the exact moment that the huge heaving ferry boat had descended far enough in the swell for the ship's car-ramp at the rear of the vessel, to be in conjunction with the edge of the harbour. Well more or less.

"ALLEZ!" they shouted in unison.

At which moment the white-faced car driver, and his equally white-faced passengers, shot onto the car deck.

"Bloody brilliant," recalled Denis, "Bloody French!"

Eddie had spent that particular crossing trying out the various sick bags, which the crew had been commanded to distribute around the constantly rolling vessel. It was it seems Capitaine Jules's only concession to the 'mother of all storms', which was presently venting its anger in the port of Plymouth. But Eddie's unfortunate reaction to, "a little bit of turbulence." as Denis had described it, wasn't the only memorable feature of that particular voyage.

Oh no! For the girls, the highlight of that eventful night had definitely been the glistening stevedores who were directing the traffic onto the boat. Though perfectly contented with their compliant husbands, it didn't from time to time, stop the 'gals' from flirting with any youngish male who might catch their eye with a smile or a wink, or possibly just having crossed their path. It was all innocent and in good fun but competition between them could at times add a dangerous element and, on the odd occasion lead to some close shaves. On this particular occasion, it had been the sight of the 'wet-look' gang of well-ripped bronze and French stevedores, that had distracted them from fully appreciating the possible consequences of a mistimed, 'Allez'.

That possibility, however, had not been lost on Denis.

"In fairness." he recalled mischievously. "We were all a bit 'distracted' on that crossing, eh girls?"

To which Gloria rather randomly added. "Yeh and the main reason Eddie was ill was the six pints of lager on top of that egg mayonnaise baguette."

"Thank you friends." said Eddie, attempting to get the conversation back to the here and now.

"Don't you just love it Denis, when even your wife…, anyway as I was saying." he continued.

"It's not just a sail on a boat, it's a day of incomparable adventure on the 'Maid d'Aquitaine', a schooner or something, including snorkelling and swimming with dolphins. It also includes a special maritime meal experience and romantic cocktails at sunset, before returning to our berth. That's back to shore Gloria. I googled it, the trip, not the word, it sounds great. What do you think? Look, here's a brochure I picked up from over there."

"Snorkelling! You can forget that one." was Maisie's response.

"And you can keep your dolphins." added Gloria for good measure. "I'm not having those things prodding and poking me, everything in the sea bites."

"Mind you." Maisie unexpectedly continued, "Spending a day on a boat, under a sun-shade, drinking cocktails, might not be that bad after all."

"Well it doesn't appeal to me one bit." intervened Gloria, "you don't have to clean up after that idiot and ….ah," she said, trailing off, having clocked a glimpse of the leaflet in Maisie's hand, and more to the point, the smiling face of Earnest, the Aquitaine's handsome skipper, beaming out from the front cover of the said brochure.

Denis was a little taken aback by his wife's sudden change of heart, and was suitably intrigued, at least until it was his turn to view the tourist pamphlet, when he realised the reason for both their wives' sudden conversion. Unperturbed, he launched into his lecture.

"Ah, Eleanour of Aquitaine." said Denis. "Ah yes, the region of Aquitaine used to belong to the English crown in the middle ages." he added casually, "or" he muttered to himself, "was that where the Popes lived? Or was that Avignon? Yeh, that's right. Yeh Aqui…."

But when he looked up, they'd gone.

"Bloody morons." he said bitterly.

The marvellous looking 'Maid d'Aquitaine', named after Eleanour, who on inheriting her father's vast estates at the tender age of fifteen, and thus becoming the most sought-after bride in French history, certainly did her namesake proud.

Petite but perfectly formed, the vessel dominated the harbour side, not with her size but with her elegance and beauty.

"Wow!!" was the general consensus.

Their communal trance was broken by the sound of the melodic tones of Earnest, who had spied the four potential customers. His magnificent frame radiant in the sunshine blazing behind him.

"Would you like ze trip on ze beautiful Eleanor laideeze, and of course, gentle mans?"

"Where do I sign?" thought Maisie

"Erm, well, how much is ze, er the, the trip, please?" enquired Denis.

Denis, initially in concert with his mate Eddie's enthusiasm, was addressing the more prosaic question of cost. It was the only occasion when his romantic side lost out to more mundane concerns.

"Well of course, it is an whole day trip, ze food and ze wine, ze cocktails, ze maritime experiences."

"Here we go." thought Denis, "And ze bloody big bill."

"For you lovely laidees, and of course your companions, sixty euros each person. For ze experience you will not forget."

"Cor blimey." calculated Denis, "that's only about fifty quid. Mind you that's a hundred for both of us, that's today's budget blown and a bit more besides, but that's food and….."

Denis didn't finish his ruminating before the girls finished it for him, and Eddie, who had spotted a couple of fishing rods on the boat, was also already sold on the idea.

"Sounds great to me." he chipped in.

"Good, tomorrow 10am sharp, just 'ere." he said, before adding with a flourish,

"Enchantées et au revoir Mesdames. Et Messieurs, of course."

"Oh yes, enchanted." Maisie managed to splutter.

Gloria just stared.

The gals had once again been hopelessly seduced by the charm of yet another handsome male with a foreign accent. It didn't help any resistance that they may have mustered had they wanted to, that what he lacked in youthfulness, he made up for with his sheer rugged weather-worn stature.

"A character straight out of Aristotle's Mediterranean Odysseys." mused Maisie.

"A mixture of olive oil and that chibatto thing." added Gloria.

So that is how, on a beautiful September day, the four companions found themselves on board the 'Maid d'Aquitaine', setting out into the vast deep blue waters of the Mediterranean sea, and in the safe hands of Earnest, the handsomest sailor the girls had ever seen, well, since the last one.

As they sailed out of the confines of the pretty stone harbour, the sea was calm, the wind light, and their spirits high. What on earth could possibly go wrong? Oh come on, Denis was with them for a start!

Several days earlier, the beautiful town of Villefranche, a veritable jewel in the Mediterranean coastline, had seemed just the place to launch into the sparkling waters of the Med. And so it would have been, had Denis in his excitement, not misread the road signs.

Always determined whilst behind the wheel of a vehicle to avoid being usurped by his annoyingly efficient wife, Denis was happy that, along with Gloria, she had fallen asleep quite early on this journey. Gloria, though not generally having a lot to offer in the navigational department, was always ready to support her friend when Maisie pointed out Denis's directional errors. Eddie, who was supposed to be Denis's co-pilot, wasn't much of a help either, though to be fair, due to Denis's parsimony, he was aided solely by a copy of a road map of France, which unfortunately ran out just before Villefranche. Denis's frugality could at times border on the obsessive, which on occasion could have unfortunate consequences. This was just such an occasion.

Denis had decided, that shelling out 10 Euros for another map, when it was obvious where Villefranche was located, was quite unnecessary. But now he had to put up with Eddie sarcastically pointing out that, having left the map, which he had spread out in front of him as best he could, they were now somewhere on the dashboard. Ho ho. This was neither helpful or in the circumstances funny. It got even worse, when awoken from her slumbers by the scent of her dear husband's discomfort, Maisie yawned and casually declared,

"We're lost aren't we Denis?"

"How the hell does she do that?" thought Denis.

"Well not really my love." he replied, without much confidence.

"So where are we then Denis dear?" Maisie continued, sensing blood.

"Tell them where we are Eddie. Oh no, don't bother. Yes, we are a bit dear."

Disturbed from her own siesta by Maisie's sudden rise in temperature, Gloria helpfully joined in with,

"Ah, you haven't lost us again have you Denis?"

"I should be so lucky." thought Denis.

"No we just have to…." but before he could finish his sentence and just as Maisie was about to deliver the coup de grace by reminding him of her previous warnings regarding maps, past experiences and false economy, a road sign appeared and writ large upon it was the word,

'Cannes'

"Oh wow!!!" Gloria managed to gasp. "Film Festival, Cat Walk, St Tropez, French Riviera, George Clooney, Celebrity Parties."

What collocations did Gloria not manage to come up with?

Goodbye reasonably priced chambre d'hotes Denis.

"Oh Denis, you are such a tease." said the merciless Maisie. "and all along you were bringing us to the French Riviera!!!"

"The French Riviera." they both chimed in unison, "WOW!!!"

"Oh gawd." muttered Denis. "Yes." he laughed weakly. "Such a pair of teasers aren't we? Eh Eddie?"

Eddie, ever so slightly confused, just grinned.

As usual, Denis found himself in between a rock and a hard place, and both of them were his wife. He could try to repair his position by stopping and regrouping and hopefully finding the direction to Villefranche, but hesitated at suggesting that, because of a fear of death. Alternatively, he could continue with this game in which he had surprised them all by delivering them to the French Riviera.

The second option, though seriously hitting his pocket, did not necessarily involve serious injury to his person, so despite the damage to his carefully planned budget, he went for that one. This option was also received with unanimous and unbridled joy by his companions, and so, courtesy of Denis, here they were in beautiful Cannes, this jewel of the Riviera.

Maisie did feel a little twinge of sympathy, poor Denis, he was trying his best, and she did feel his pain. But Denis, how many times....

At '10am sharp' they had arrived at the berth of the 'Maid d'Aquitaine'. For Denis, the prospect of a day out on the glistening blue waters of the Mediterranean Sea, or indeed any sea did appeal, and so it would have been churlish of him not to join in the excitement at the prospect of swimming and snorkelling around the clear reefs of their destination, les Iles de Lerins. Consisting of a group of islands just off the coast of Cannes, les Iles, they were informed were, "just a short ten-minute skoot from the harbour." and consisted of the main one, Ile Sainte Marguerite and Ile Saint-Honorat.

Despite the rather business-like reception from Captain Earnest, which after the previous day's performance came as a bit of a surprise, their spirits were high. It was certainly a bit of a cold shower moment when on boarding the beautiful Maid d'Aquitaine the excited Brits were met with,

'Ze rules.'

It seemed that any romantic notions regarding Earnest, which the two rivals in love, may have harboured, would have on this occasion been left back in the harbour. However at the conclusion of Earnest's masterful performance regarding, 'ze rules', they were well and truly back on board.

"I 'ave ze, ow you say, an allergy of ze suntan cream." began Earnest.

"How weird." thought Maisie.

But as if by magic and right on cue, Denis with what seemed to be a pre-rehearsed routine, provided the explanation by way of a live performance. Leaning his hand on the seat at the side of the boat he immediately slipped onto the floor.

"That's your bloody fault" he muttered to Maisie as he flapped around trying to restore his dignity.

"What?"

"For getting me to do your back before we got on board."

Maisie, along with the rest of the occupants of the boat, struggled not to slip onto the floor herself, but it was more to do with laughing than suntan lotion.

"And your name is?"

"Er, Denis." replied Denis, feeling a bit like a schoolboy.

"Hmm, trooble." observed Earnest, his left eyebrow pointing skywards.

"Now." continued Earnest, no longer the ever so slightly flirty bronzed medallion of the previous day. But now very much the Master of his craft.

"Zeez are ze rules. All sun tan cream goes into zis bas ket along wiz ze mobil pherns."

"Ferns?" whispered Eddie

"Ferns?" shrugged Denis

"Phones. Idiots." said Maisie, helpfully.

"Do you finished? May I continue?" enquired a very solemn-faced Earnest.

"If we leave ze seat to move around ze boat we always hold onto something, but not someone. Is zat clear?"

"Don't left wet towls on ze fleur. If you want someone to fall."

"That's 'unless', 'unless', you want someone to fall." thought Denis smugly.

"Always listen to your skipper and do as told."

"Finally. All members of ze crew, zat's you, will do all activities."

"Some bloody chance." thought Maisie, "I ain't snorkelling."

Gloria was smitten and stared straight ahead at Earnest, having heard very little of ze rules.

"Excuse me." ventured Maisie. "Erm, I can't put my face in water, I can't do that."

"And your name is?"

"Erm Maisie, Maisie Wilson."

"Well Maisie Wilson we will see." he said, with a warm smile. Maisie immediately melted and almost wanted to plunge her face into a bucket of water right there and then.

Despite his rather brusque manner and the uncompromising delivery of his rules and regs, Earnest could not hide his Gallic charm which seemed, at least as far as the ladies were concerned, to ooze out like a tube of sun cream on a hot day. His shiny bronze six feet plus stature helped too.

In fact, as soon as the mandatory health and safety announcement was over Earnest slipped effortlessly back into the role of the charming skipper and host.

"Bloody showman." thought Denis.

"If you good people will allow we will ed for ze smaller off ze big islands. He is called Ile Saint-Honorat and he has some little ones too behind him, perfect for snorkelling. But first, we will all swim."

"Apparently there are sea caves and tunnels where we can go exploring with our snorkels." said Denis, excitedly.

"Great." responded Eddie, but with a little less enthusiasm. He had in the past been a reluctant partner of Denis in ventures, which had on the surface seemed a good idea, but had often gone a little awry. This little venture didn't even begin on the surface!

"How do you know that, anyway?" he inquired, quietly impressed with Denis's knowledge.

"Oh I don't know." said Denis nonchalantly, "Just something I knew." he added, as he slipped his towel over the pamphlet on the seat.

"We might meet some trolls." added Eddie trying to sound more in concert with his mate.

"Nah, they're too busy rubbishing peoples' books." retorted Dennis cryptically.

Arriving at a small sandy bay, Earnest told them that it was time for a swim, no snorkelling just yet, he knew a far more suitable place for that. The sea was a beautiful aquamarine blue, and though the water was deep you could just about make out the bottom far below. It was also very warm and inviting. The boys already wearing their bathers under their shorts were soon ready to plunge in and would have immediately if Maisie hadn't suddenly said,

"Your back Denis?"

 "Yes, my little Angel cake?" said Denis

"And the top of your head Denis." Maisie added cruelly.

"I did Eddie's before we got on while Denis was doing yours Maise, so Eddie's good to go." chipped in Gloria. "But actually I don't think there's much cream left….. Oh there isn't any."

"You did bring our bottle didn't you Denis? You know the one in the beach bag?"

"We aren't at the beach my love."

Maisie didn't bother with a response.

"You haven't packed a spare in your bag have you Eddie?" enquired Denis hopefully. But a huge spout of water told him that Eddie, his mate, couldn't wait.

"Cheers mate!"

"You'll have to wear your vest Denis, and fortunately Clare has lent us her swimming cap, so you can put that on to protect your pate, mate." she said holding up a bright pink bathing cap.

Earnest, observing the curiously English pantomime smiled wryly, he did love the Brits, they were always such fun.

"Great, just great." muttered Denis, as he edged his way to the end of the boat.

Although not quite managing to cut it as a member of the sophisticated St Tropez jet set, he was trying his best not to look like a 'Brit abroad', but this wasn't helped when he kind of slipped, dived and fell into the crystal clear waters, all at the same time. Still, once he was in everything was forgotten, except that he had forgotten how bad sea water tasted and spent most of the time spitting out every time he neglected to keep his mouth closed. But it was superb.

Back on the boat, Gloria was trying unsuccessfully, to convince Maisie to take the plunge. Choosing a clever ploy to reassure her by saying that the depth of the water wasn't an issue, as you could drown in much less water than that, Earnest eventually had to come to the rescue. Producing a swimming aid, which, once he had securely attached to Maisie's torso, convincing her that she was safe, she began to relent. But she wasn't putting her face in, no bloody way.

Gloria though not by any means a natural athlete was when it came to water, like the proverbial fish, and slipped in like a mermaid. It really was a superb beginning to what promised to be a wonderful day's sailing.

Whilst the 'crew-mates' swam, Earnest was on a mission of his own. Silhouetted by the blazing sun behind him, he appeared dramatically on the prow of the boat. Bedecked modestly in an exotically colourful African printed wrap-around skirt, which he whipped off to reveal his standard-issue skimpy French speedos, he stretched his arms up skywards and plunged into the water like a dolphin. Gloria, treading water with her mouth agape, managed to gasp,

 "Will you look at that!!"

At the same time, poor Maisie, being wrongly positioned, struggled to turn her head in response, and then nearly went belly up in the process of trying.

Diving down for what felt like an age, Earnest finally appeared with what seemed to be a bag in his hand.

"Wow! Where the hell did he have that hidden?" thought Gloria.

"Hmm, I think I've an idea." muttered Denis to himself.

But it was the contents of the bag that were to prove even more amazing.

After a good swim and the inevitable 'game' of diving and surfacing under the very nervous Maisie, for which she assured Denis he would later pay, the group began to reassemble at the ladder at the stern of the boat. Earnest was already back on board and busy with the first of the day's culinary treats.

Greeting them as they hauled themselves up the steel steps, was a fold-away table packed with a wonderful assortment of locally sourced Provençal foods. Sun-dried tomatoes, local cheeses, tapenade made from finely chopped anchovies, olives, capers and olive oil, chunks of fresh baguette, a pot of steaming bouillabaisse, dips and spreads, prosciutto and a huge selection of green and black olives. As they stared hungrily at the table, Earnest appeared from the galley below.

"Not yet my friends first we hef ze beautiful prowns."

"Where the hell did all that lot come from?"

"Cor blimey, there's more to this guy than meets the eye, eh girls?" quipped Eddie.

Earnest was carrying a huge pan of freshly cooked prawns seasoned with garlic and lemon. After squeezing them into a space in the middle of the table, he invited them all to sit down.

"Now we can eat!" he declared.

"But first we drunk an toast. To the beautiful creatures of the sea." he said looking shamelessly at the girls. Cue silly giggles.

"Cor, pass the bucket Eddie." responded Denis.

The table did not take long to empty, even Maisie, who preferred her seafood on a plate, or even better, wrapped in paper, joined in with enthusiasm. Their early morning swim had certainly whetted their appetites, and with encouragement from Earnest, she even tucked into the juicy "prowns."

The veritable banquet that their host had spread before them, though impressive, had not included the contents of the mysterious bag which had magically appeared after Earnest's lengthy dive into the crystal waters surrounding the boat. It seemed that this 'little spread' was merely the prelude to the main event.

After ensuring that the stage was clear and ready for Act II, he once again disappeared into the galley, returning moments later with the bag, which he unceremoniously emptied onto the table. The lack of any prelude only served to heighten the expectation which was signalled by the gasps of amazement at the appearance of the huge smorgasbord of creatures from the deep, spread out before them.

Dragged from their repose under the safe havens of the various cracks and crevices afforded by the rocky seabed, the shocked collection of molluscs and crustaceans seemed to blink in the bright sunlight. But this was no vulgar, "Bon apetit and tuck in." This was a carefully choreographed presentation, a celebration of the cornucopia of culinary delights yielded by the magnanimous waters of the Mediterranean. Earnest's sea.

With the emotion clearly audible in his voice, Earnest declared,

"Zis my friends, iz my gift to you today. The abundant fruits of my companion and first lurv, ze ocean."

"Cor get on with it." thought Denis irreverently, "I want to go bloody snorkelling."

The girls, smitten, stared, their eyes glistening.

After accompanying our four companions through the consumption of the mostly recognisable, if not commonly ingested collection of sea creatures, Earnest produced the final offering. Sitting in the middle of the table, and covered in a carpet of algae, was what appeared to be a medium-sized rock. Denis, who distracted with thoughts of snorkelling, had up to this point only been vaguely paying attention, now sat up at the sight of Earnest drawing his knife across the 'rock' and opening up a beautifully vibrant orange interior with what appeared to be a large fleshy creature at its centre.

"Gosh!" he whispered to Eddie. "That's an abalone, a haliotis tuberculata if I am not mistaken. Bloody Hell, he must have dived down to at least four meters to get that. Bloody Hell!"

"Zis my friends is ze queen of ze deep, I preesent to you zee magnifique, ormeau."

"Yep, abalone." concurred Denis, "Told you so, bloody 'ell!"

"And now." declared Earnest, unperturbed by Denis's stage whispers.

"A queen for ze queen." as he handed the open shell to Maisie. At which point Gloria's transfixed gaze became ever so slightly, un-transfixed.

"Why her?" she thought, "She doesn't even eat seafood."

Maisie, equally entranced by Earnest's performance, and who had up to this point been dutifully consuming the kind of offering that she would normally gag at, nervously received this latest offering in her hand with appropriate reverence, she was even about to dispatch it, when Earnest stopped her,

"Wait! Ze lemon juice."

"Ceviche." again whispered Denis, knowingly. It's a way of cooking shellfish using lemon juice."

"Oh yeh." replied Eddie, trying to sound impressed.

Earnest leant over and squeezed the juice onto the unsuspecting abalone which immediately responded by kicking and screaming all over its shell.

"Now into ze mouse, you will feel ze tingle and zen down."

Maisie, by now ever so slightly unentranced, managed to get the thing into her 'mouse' and then hesitated at the tingle,

"Kill it! Kill it!" Earnest barked.   And she did and swallowed it.

"Hm, dodged a bullet there." thought Gloria peevishly.

"Yuk!" thought Eddie.

Denis, who was already a little bit put out at the fact that despite the very enjoyable fayre provided by Earnest, it had not included any alcoholic beverage, was even more miffed when 'Ze snorkelling' had to be delayed until their lunch had settled.

"Cor blimey, it'll be dark before we get to explore properly." he moaned to Eddie.

An ashen-faced Maisie was more than content to sit quietly, not wishing to display ingratitude by returning the contents of her stomach back into the ocean from whence it had come.

Eddie, equally raring to get going, sympathised with his pal but did point out with a pleased grin that there was probably zero tolerance in France for, 'Ze drinking and diving'.

Eventually Earnest sanctioned the adventure beneath the sea, and after quickly explaining the equipment, i.e. mask, snorkel and flippers, before giving a dire warning about the importance of being careful of 'ze' sea urchins, they were good to go.

Unfortunately due to his impatience to get going, Denis had paid little attention to Earnest's health and safety talk, and sadly his enthusiasm for snorkelling not being matched by any kind of proficiency meant that despite several changes of mask, he couldn't seem to get the hang of how you stopped the "bloody thing" filling with water. By the time he had reached an acceptable degree of competence, his snorkelling companion had once again taken off without him.

"Bloody charming." he thought. "And it was my idea to do the snorkelling and exploring the sea caves together in the first place."

The idea of snorkelling on his own didn't seem so attractive.

Meanwhile, with the intention of getting her to attempt snorkelling, Maisie, now fully recovered from her own lunchtime adventure, was slowly being coaxed by Earnest into entering the water wearing a snorkel. Previously adamant that it "ain't gonna happen", she was now, with Earnest's close attention, slowly warming to the possibility, and when he invited her to,

"Lay ze tummy across my 'ands and I will gently lower you into ze water." Maisie's phobia began to recede quicker than an ebbing spring tide.

In fact, by the time Earnest had completed his gentle coaching, her resistance had been overcome, and she spent the rest of the afternoon, literally like a fish in water swimming around the boat, face down and marvelling at the marine landscape below.

Some distance away, as Maisie had laid across Earnest's supportive 'ands' repeatedly asking, if he could just,

"...take me through that one more time."

Gloria fumed,

"Why didn't I come across as pathetic?"

Denis was truly marvelling at the magnificent sites below and had occasionally ventured deeper to get a closer look, but after accidentally trying to breathe-in, whilst his snorkel was still submerged, he was now exercising a little more caution. He was considering going back towards the boat to look for Eddie when he decided that though he wasn't going to explore on his own, he would take a look at the entrance to the sea caves which were tantalisingly close.

Wishing he had 'bothered' with the flippers, another result of his impatience, he swam as fast as he could towards the rock face, which despite his efforts, didn't seem to be getting much closer. Eventually, in a state of some fatigue, he arrived at the gaping mouth of one of the caves. Ominously dark and narrower than he had imagined, he held on to the side of the rock, and carefully leaned around to see if he could get a better look.

WHOOOOSH!! Off he went straight down the tunnel carried along on an irresistible gush of water that was being sucked through the narrow channel. On he went incapable of any kind of resistance using his hands to prevent crashing into the side and conscious of avoiding hitting his head on the rock face above.

"Bloody Hell!" he thought. "What a way to go! And they'll never find my body. So much for donating my kidneys."

It was just as it occurred to him that he hadn't breathed since the beginning of his unscheduled trip along the tunnel and that this may soon present a problem, that he suddenly found himself being spewed out and tumbling into a huge water-filled cavern.

Coughing, spluttering, no mask, no snorkel, but still alive, Denis gazed around at the surrounding rock faces towering above, all covered with algae, just like the unfortunate abalone that had been ignominiously dispatched earlier.

"One life for another." he mused, pondering his fate, "How apposite, how fitting, how poetic. How very, shit!"

It was then that it dawned on him that for some reason he could actually see his surroundings. Looking up, way above, there was a shaft of sunlight bursting through the hole in the cave roof. Although it was far too high to consider climbing up the treacherous rock face, it at least gave him hope, though he wasn't sure why.

"That's what geologists call a chimney, I believe." he thought to himself, as you would in this situation.

He had hardly begun to question the rationale for the 'hope', when in the water ahead of him, just where it seemed to disappear on its onward journey through the tunnels, there was a significant disturbance.

"Oh great." he thought, "a giant water snake. I've heard of those in Borneo."

Resigned to his new fate, he attempted to manoeuvre himself back to the relative safety of a glistening rock, when a head popped up.

"Oh hi Denis. What are you doing here?"

"Fishing Eddie, fishing mate."

It took a while for Eddie to convince Denis that despite not having a mask and snorkel, the journey back to the surface, after an initial tricky few feet, would be relatively safe, as he could keep his head above the water for most of the way, and that the flow, in the same way as it had 'helped' him to get in, would equally help him to get out. Looking up at the shaft of sunlight way above, the gush of water cascading into the basin behind, and recognising the onset of hypothermia, Denis realised that in terms of options, as usual, there really weren't that many to choose from, actually only one.

Taking a huge breath they plunged into the swirling tide of the out going tunnel, and, as Eddie had promised, they were soon swiftly being carried along towards the safety of the cave entrance. Using their legs to guide themselves along the tunnel walls, the boys were making excellent progress. As the entrance approached and the darkness began to recede, Denis was even beginning to enjoy the ride.

Unfortunately, without his mask, Denis didn't have a chance of spotting the sea, AAAHHHHHHHAAAHHHHHHH!!!!!!!! urchin, on which he had inadvertently placed his foot.

As the excruciating pain reeled through his whole body, his head instinctively shot back, smashing against the tunnel roof. And that's all he remembered.

◆ ◆ ◆

Denis, before drifting back into oblivion, managed to mumble, the first time….

"Where am I? Who is it? What am I? Where are we? What's going on…..?"

On the second occasion. "How is it? Where are we? What's going on?"

And the third, "What am I doing here? Huh, what you doing here Maisie? Why aren't you on the boat?"

Denis's dutiful wife, always by his side, decided that this latest utterance finally merited a response.

"Well Denis," she replied sardonically. "You're here because you are here, and I am here because I have come to see the Jaques Cousteau tribute act, which is supposed to be appearing in town. That would be you Denis."

Denis, exhausted by this conversation was about to drift back into oblivion when nurse Veronique came in to check on her very own, 'English Patient'.

Ever since going on a school trip to London when she was ten years old, which had included a visit to see the pantomime 'Dick Whittington', Veronique had desperately wanted to call someone, a 'Silly Billy'. At last, here he was, and finally awake.

"Monsieur Wil Son. Ow are you? You Silly Billy!"

"Oh Gawd." was all he managed in response before drifting off again.

Maisie and Veronique raised their collective eyebrows in unison to the ceiling.

❖ ❖ ❖

"Poor Denis." opined Gloria, back on the 'Maid d'Aquitaine'.

"Lucky Denis more like." corrected Eddie.

"Poor Maisie." she added with a slight glint in her eye, as she sank her third Margarita and nuzzled up closer to Earnest. Sadly though, it was all one-way traffic.

Eddie, hoping to catch a big one, was too busy sorting out his fishing tackle to notice anyway.

"You're not the Queen of the Seas now are you Maisie Wilson? Boom! Boom!" (Ouch.)

◆ ◆ ◆

Back at the Centre Hospitalier de Cannes, nurse Veronique was just beginning her final round of the evening.

"Ello Monsieur Wil Son, it is time for your another injection for ze venom…….You Silly Billy!"

CHAPTER 3

Monsieur Marcel Couturier, known to his friends as Marcel 'ze fish', or to his enemies as Marcel 'ze thug', stood in front of his mirror admiring his gladiatorial frame.

"Today," Marcel announced, "you will prove yourself once again to be the greatest at the art of 'le peche' in the whole region of the Auvergne."

"Ze best. Peerless. Ze master of everything before you!"

"Have you finished in that bathroom yet, you great lummox?" screamed a voice.

Well, nearly everything.

"I'm not in the bathroom, ma Cherie, I am in the bedroom." he scowled.

"Well what the hell are you doing? If you think that you are going fishing before you've been to collect the post, moved that lawnmower into the back, and cleaned the kitchen sink after you have shifted that bloody pile of crap out of it, you can go whistle."

"Yes dear."

The 'pile of crap' was Marcel's latest addition to his arsenal of fishing gear. A very rare 1960's hand-made ABU ZEBCO "special foot." Cardinal 44 fishing reel 1st version. Separated into its component parts, it was presently sitting in the sink and being cleaned in a mild mix of vinegar and olive oil (yes really). It was being prepared for its lead role in the capture of the mother of all fish in the 2010 Parc Naturel Regional Livradois-Forez freshwater coarse fishing competition.

Yes the mighty Zander, terror of the deep, part perch, part pike, ferocious, predatory, dark and mysterious, a perfect adversary for Marcel 'ze thug'.

Marcel, still prickling from his dear wife's latest reminder of who ruled this particular roost, did not deal well with humiliation, but that bitch could go hang herself. It only served to fire him up for the task ahead and woe betide anybody who might get in the way of his latest inevitable triumph.

Maybe not her, but someone would pay for her venom!

"Coming, ma petite mignon." he snarled.

With a final glance in the mirror to admire that chiselled face, well-worn by a combination of Calvados, black tobacco and age, he picked up his green baize fishing hat and breezed out of the bedroom en route to his glorious destiny which today, absolutely nothing and nobody would get in the way of.

◆ ◆ ◆

Denis, in response to the gentle rise in temperature of the tent, was stirring. His wife Maisie sensing danger i.e. her husband being awake, greeted him sweetly with her unique version of 'good morning',

"If you wake me up Denis, I will kill you."

"Just putting the kettle on, my sweetie pie. Well not actually putting it on." he chuckled to himself.

Yes, 'gleeful Denis', was in his usual early morning mood and why not? The sun was already shining on the wonderful campsite, to which the previous night, and whilst it was still light, Denis had successfully delivered his companions.

A gossamer-thin layer of early morning dew sparkled on the grass, the air was fresh and clear and Denis was at peace with the world. Even Maisie, after swallowing a somewhat large portion of humble pie, conceded that Denis had indeed exceeded expectations in his role as the party's driver.

And so on this glorious French morning what better way was there to continue this wonderful start than with a nice cup of, 'Rosie Lee', as Eddie would say. He also realised that the promise of a brew was the only way he would see his wife, or indeed, any of his camping companions, in 'active' mode on this side of noon-hour.

Denis though not strictly nocturnal, had, at least as others saw it, been afflicted by an inability to sleep once light had appeared on the horizon. Not too bad on long dark nights of winter but as you can imagine in summer, oh dear. Unfortunately Denis's genuine attempts to 'get on with it' quietly, never really worked either, so it wasn't long before other heads began appearing. If he ever felt that they needed assistance in vacating their sleeping bags he would, in a weird twist on a macabre horror film he had once seen, direct the spout of the coffee pot into the inner tents of slumbering occupants. In the film, it had been carbon monoxide from a car, but coffee was just as good and obviously safer.

Pretty soon, first Eddie, then Gloria, Clare, Jack and eventually his beloved wife, having had her resolve finally broken, appeared in their various states of consciousness. It was also invaluable in moving things along if he had already hatched a plan for the day and today he was ready, oh boy was he ever.

Wasting no more time he announced confidently.

"Un plan d'eau loisir! You know a recreational lake, beach, swimming, water sports,……and…and," glancing towards Eddie, "Fishing!!"

Each member of the party had perked up at some point during the announcement, each one imagining the possibilities of, sunbathing on a sandy beach, flying down ridiculously long water slides or landing that enormous mother of all giant trouts. Eddie was beside himself with excitement, the possibility of trying out that new fishing gear that he had bought for a bargain off eBay. And the girls, well they were already back in the tents searching out their various lotions.

"Hold on. Hold on." Maisie said suddenly hesitating, as she remembered to factor Denis's map reading skills into the general excitement.

"Where is it? How far is it? What time will we get there?"

Denis, having done his homework, responded confidently,

"Well I am very glad you asked, Maisie. Parc Naturel Regional Livradois-Forez, is a mere ten kilometres from this very campsite!"

"So at least two hours." thought Maisie cruelly. But even her well-founded caution couldn't stem the universal enthusiasm and within half an hour and in very high spirits, they were on their way.

What could possibly go wrong? Oh come on!

◆ ◆ ◆

Marcel still smarting from his wife's outburst which had delayed his departure was wasting no time as his battered old Renault 4 van tore around the winding lanes of the Puy de Dome on its way to lac Aubussond, Auvergne. Whilst tearing around one particular tight bend he was not best pleased when he was confronted by a vehicle with English number plates heading straight at him…. but then neither was Denis coming the other way.

"Oh Gawd, a French driver travelling with even less care than usual."

"This'll be fun." observed Gloria.

"You'll have to back up Denis." advised Maisie, helpfully.

"Well one of us will." suggested Denis, bravely.

"Denis!"

"OK, OK. Why is it always me?" he muttered under his breath.

Denis's attempts to back his rather large and heavily laden camper round narrow bends did not go smoothly and the four passengers in the back who were trying to help by bobbing up and down contributed very little to his ability to see where he was going. By the time he had managed to pull into a passing place, whilst at the same time inadvertently drifting over to the wrong side of the road, Marcel was reaching new levels of rage. As he squeezed his battered van through the gap he leaned over menacingly. Denis as well as smelling the pungent aroma of anger and garlic was close enough to feel the heat of his breath as Marcel screamed,

"Connard!!"

"Ass hole!!!!" Denis retorted just as Marcel, though still in earshot, was a safe distance away.

"Dennis!!!" chided a shocked Maisie. Gloria had to look out of the window.

Sending out a belch of black smoke, Marcel who on this occasion had more important matters to attend to, roared off, but he would not forget the smug face of that English, 'cretin' and when he saw the raised finger in his mirror he was tempted to go back and rearrange it there and then.

By the time Denis had found his way around the winding lanes Maisie's two hours had proved slightly optimistic and as they pulled into the muddy space between the road and the lake, which they only recognised as a carpark because it had lots of cars on it, the 'high spirits' of the morning had dissipated into the usual acceptance that life with Denis the tour guide, could be a very hit and miss affair.

"Well we have found the lake." he managed to utter positively. "But sadly not the water park." he conceded under his breath.

"And why so many cars, and no people? Spooky."

Maisie, with a gentle shake of the head and a gasp of frustration, was already, along with the rest of the crew, too resigned to the inevitable to even respond.

"It's the hope that kills you." she lamented.

"Well I am desperate for the loo." said Gloria and slamming the door in frustration, she headed off to the cover of a reed bed at the edge of the lake.

"You comin' Maise?" she shouted.

At that moment and without the presence of an accompanying breeze the dense vegetation around the 'car-park' began to rustle mysteriously.

"Oh great! That mad French guy has followed us." thought Denis half-seriously.

"Might as bloody well." shouted back Maisie. And as she set off to follow her companion she gave the door another good slam which this time prompted even more evident disturbance in the undergrowth, accompanied by a series of strange cries,

"ZUT ALOR!!"

"MON DIEU!!"

Denis and his companions looked at each other nervously.

"You coming Clare?"

"You must be joking, I'm not going in the bushes, anyway this place is creeping me out."

Undaunted by any strange goings-on in the bushes, Gloria strode on, well as best she could.

"When you gotta go you gotta go." she thought.

"Look we could go over there behind those reeds Maise." she said, pointing vaguely in the direction of a little clearing in the undergrowth.

"That mud looks solid enough."

Denis was ruminating as to what his best option was going forward. It was always better to be proactive in these situations, for instance, pretend that this was a planned comfort break which the girls had naturally taken full advantage of and that he knew exactly where the leisure park was, which he didn't, and that was a worry. 'Eddie the navigator', as Denis had wryly observed, was too engrossed in his guide book, 'Fishing in the Auvergne', to be of much assistance,

"Yeh typical everyone relies on me, 'ideas man Denis', but as soon as the slightest thing goes wrong you're on your own mate, it's burn him at the bloody stake time."

"Any thoughts Eddie?"

"Huh? Yeh you know the zander, that's a fish in these parts, lurks in the deep volcanic lakes and can reach 20 kilos!! Lovely fish to eat too apparently, all meaty and white. Hey if we aren't doing anything I'll bale out here it looks like a decent place to fish."

Denis was just about to thank Eddie for his support when they heard a scream from the lake shore. Gloria's solid enough mud wasn't solid enough after all, and having already reached her knees she was well along the process of sinking deeper into it.

"Eddieee!!!"

"Wow!" said Eddie reaching for his camcorder, "Wow! 'You've Been Framed'!"

To the accompaniment of doors slamming, people screaming and even more mysterious sounds coming from deep in the shrubbery, a head, festooned in the wardrobe afforded by the local flora, suddenly and gracefully, rose out of the undergrowth.

In his twenty-seven years as a member of, and the last two as 'Le President' of the 'Puy du Dome Avian Observation Association', Monsieur Gilbert La Fayette, had spent many hours crawling around in bushes in pursuit of elusive quarry and during that time had stumbled across some very odd sights. However never as odd as this one. He would in later years recount to stunned members of the Avian Association's AGM, how on that particular August day whilst in pursuit of the elusive Slovenian grebe, apparently due in any time soon, he had been shocked to observe, a hysterical female sinking slowly into a cess-pit of mud, accompanied by another equally hysterical female screaming at a seemingly motionless male apparently trapped in a state of inertia, with two young people staring on in a mixture of wonder and concern but most incredible of all, a second male filming the whole scene with a camcorder! As he had also remarked sagely to his companions at the time,

"Les Anglais. Ooh La la!!"

"Ah les Anglais." chorused a host of enlightened twitchers, "Oui oui, les Anglais."

It had not been a good day for the association. It had started badly with the arrival of the local fishing fraternity whose annual freshwater competition happened this year to clash with the arrival of the Slovenian grebe. Their raucous and bellicose behaviour had probably sent the poor thing scurrying back from whence it had come. And now this. As the series of camouflaged heads descended back into hiding, Eddie, realising that his dear wife was getting shorter ever so quickly decided that it was time to stop filming and that he had better do something, pretty sharpish.

Grabbing a rope from the back of the camper he threw it at her hitting her in the face but forgetting to hold on to the other end. Cue more hysterical screaming. Denis finally emerging from his trance managed to unearth a huge sapling and thrust it towards Gloria. Eventually and with the help of everyone pulling, they succeeded in extricating her from the mud.

A while later after Denis had inevitably been blamed for bringing them there in the first place, (he hadn't bothered with his 'toilet break' idea), a relative calm had been restored. Gloria however refused to go anywhere until she had washed all the mud off her legs. Unfortunately having suffered a practical physics lesson in the power of suction, Gloria's footwear had not accompanied her feet in their liberation from the mud, at least not both of them. Gloria quite often clueless, was now also shoeless and the comical sight of her hobbling around with as much dignity as she could muster was not lost on Denis. He was desperately attempting to suppress a grin in case Maisie spotted him but then he noticed his dear wife trying to do the same and which made him feel much better. Gloria oblivious to the entertainment she was providing was 'clip clopping' her way down to the lake with a bar of soap.

"And you'd better retrieve that soddin' bloody shoe Eddie!!" she screamed as she disappeared around the shrubbery

But Eddie, having realised that it was probably prudent not to announce his departure, had taken advantage of his wife's absence and had already slipped off in search of a suitable place to do some fishing. Anyway he figured Gloria's mood would be far better improved when he came back with some lovely fresh rainbow trout for tea.

"I'll see you later." he managed to whisper to Denis. "Tell her I'll buy her another pair, that should work! Pick me up here when you have finished at the park…" before adding peevishly,

"If you ever find it!".

Denis ignored Eddie's last remark and was buoyed up ever so slightly by the distinct sounds of screaming children drifting down from the other end of the lake, Denis confidently instructed Eddie to be back at the carpark no later than six o'clock. Checking the time, he optimistically reckoned that they could still get a couple of hours in at the park.

"AHH NO! I've dropped the soap dish, and its floating away!" screeched Gloria. Eddie, anticipating more drama glanced up and slipped off quietly.

When Monsieur Gilbert once again raised his head to observe this latest breach in the tranquillity he was confronted with a site which took a long time to expunge from his memory. Gloria her nether regions bedecked exclusively in her Marks and Spencer knickers, stood in the sacred nesting grounds of the Slovenian grebe with soap suds dripping off her knees and thighs. This proved to be the last straw for the bird watching fraternity. With bushes still adorning their heads Monsieur Gilbert La Fayette led the way as a disgruntled party of frustrated twitchers trudged off into their respective transport all muttering in concert,

"Les Anglais, les imbeciles."

Denis was not the only member of the party who could not hide a slight grin.

"Brilliant!" he thought. "You couldn't make it up."

◆ ◆ ◆

As Eddie rounded the final piece of bocage which separated

the winding trail from the lake shores he was met with the amazing sight of hordes of frenzied fishermen all vying for the best position to cast their fishing lines. The 2010 Parc Naturel Regional Livradois-Forez freshwater coarse fishing competition was well and truly underway. Dominating the scene and directing operations was the imposing figure of Marcel Couturier. Whilst each fisherman was being allotted a broad area in which he could stake his claim, Marcel had already established his own little exclusive fiefdom which nobody would dare to trespass upon. Despite the frenetic atmosphere, Eddie was afforded the usual polite greeting from the event's Chief Marshall, Monsieur Mureau.

"Bonjour Monsieur. Vous êtes ici pour la pêche?"

Eddie delivering an embarrassed grin and detecting an interrogative tone in the voice of his greeter, offered two of the five French words he was confident with, which usually did the trick.

"Bonjour, er oui, hm, oui."

Eddie by now had attracted the curious looks of a number of the fishing fraternity, they did not recognise this late-comer and he had a strange look about him. But with a few mutterings and a number of 'Gallic shrugs' they were far too busy to pay much attention to Eddie.

Monsieur Mureau mistaking Eddie's hesitant reply and inane grin as indicating that he must be a local simpleton from one of the villages, only recently uncovered with the advent of the Satnav, pointed to a place just around some bushes which overhung the lake, a quiet backwater where he would be, 'out of the way'. Eddie continued grinning and shuffled off around the bend, as it were, with Monsieur Mureau smiling back sympathetically.

"Well, at least I must be in a good place." Eddie mused, "these guys look as if they know what they are doing."

Wasting no time in unpacking his gear, he was soon organised and settled down to a peaceful afternoon's fishing. He loved being on holiday with Denis and Maisie but it could at times get a bit hectic, and now and again it was nice to escape for a bit of 'quiet time'.

◆ ◆ ◆

"I'm not going until I get that soap dish lid back." insisted Gloria. "I've nowhere to put my soap. It'll sticky everything."

"Oh for goodness sake Gloria we'll find a plastic bag." suggested Denis, conscious of the time and that Eddie had already been gone for nearly fifteen minutes.

"It can't have gone far Denis" Maisie chipped in helpfully. "Just have a look in those bushes it's probably only floated around that corner and got stuck."

Denis realising that as usual, he had already lost the debate before it had even really started, trudged off to the camper and pulled out a pair of wellies and whilst muttering various expletives, tramped off into the bushes bordering the water in search of,

"Gloria's bloody soap dish!"

◆ ◆ ◆

Things were swiftly hotting up at the fishing mete. There had been steady murmurs of excitement as a variety of rainbow trout, some quite big, had been landed throughout the morning. But still no zanders. Marcel whose own keep net was still empty noted ominously that rainbow trout were for women and that if any of the 'women' around him were hoping to outdo him they had better have bigger gonads than him! (Charming)

Eddie out of sight and out of mind was enjoying his own little successes. He had managed to catch three fish and even land two of them. One a decent pan-sized rainbow and one other which he had not yet identified but was a bit on the ugly side. The one that he failed to land was, of course, the largest. He was already imagining Gloria's face as he served up his rainbow trout when his imaginings were interrupted by a definite increase in the volume of the murmurings coming from upstream. The cause of the excitement was clear. Floating along the top of the water was a strange assortment of white bubbles, which were immediately recognised by the more experienced members of the fishing fraternity as the unmistakable gaseous exhalations of a very large fish! Whilst the bubbles grew in size and intensity, the excitement grew to a fever pitch as the fishermen scrambled and scrapped to gain a new position closer to the source of the phenomenon. Marcel engaged his elbows effectively and positioned himself in exactly the right place for when a huge mound of white bubbles appeared around the bend. He was also in the exact right place when a rather large piece of the very white bubbles detaching itself in the breeze from the main, floated over and landed, rather comically, on Marcel's head. The whole assembly in anticipation of his reaction took in a sharp intake of breath, but before he could respond to the very white phenomenon sitting on his head, around the bend bobbing up and down in the water, floated a very blue soap dish.

"SACRE BLEU!!!" exclaimed Marcel

"SACRE BLEU!" echoed his fellow anglers.

Just at that moment from around the main track and reverently carrying the other half of the very blue soap dish, having extricated it from a bunch of reeds, sauntered Denis. Expecting to find Eddie alone and quietly drowning worms he was taken aback by the sight of a whole host of faces staring at his soap dish as if it were the holy grail. Eddie barely had time to say,

"Hi Denis look what I..." before...

"You!" screamed Marcel, "AHHHGGGGRRRR!!!! Je vais t'arracher la tete!!!" (French for something really bad)

Denis, recognising immediately the crazy Frenchman that he had met on the road earlier that morning, also realised, immediately, that the crazy Frenchman, for some reason, was not best pleased to see him. This assessment was confirmed by Marshall, Monsieur Mureau, who informed Denis that if Monsieur Couturier said that he was going to 'rip' his head off then he probably would. Deciding that discretion was indeed the better part of valour he headed off as fast as his wellies would allow back to the relative safety of the carpark. Marcel whose incandescent rage prohibited him from interrupting the pursuit of his quarry to take off his own waders meant that his mission, i.e. to kill Denis, was somewhat hampered and inevitably lead to Denis reaching the carpark before he did.

"In the car! Get in the car! Go, go, go!!" screamed Denis at his shocked companions.

It was very rarely that Denis truly asserted himself and usually only with good reason. Recognising such a situation, the usually bullish Maisie complied immediately and off they sped. The explanations could wait.

Fortunately for Denis by the time they screeched away the remnants of the soap suds on Marcel's head had descended into his eyes and though his threats were becoming ever more lurid, he was by now blindly stumbling around in some discomfort whilst raging like a bull. Despite his blood-curdling threats he cut quite a comical figure which allowed one or two of his erstwhile enfeebled companions to even venture a quiet grin, it wasn't all bad that the mighty Marcel should be cut down to size, just a little.

Eddie, largely oblivious to the general chaos emanating from his fellow competitors upstream, was about to raise his head to see what was causing the latest disturbance when he felt the unmistakable tug of another rainbow trout, and this did feel like a big one. In fact, when his rod nearly shot out of his hands he realised that he had actually hooked the 'one that got away'!

"Blimey," he thought, "Gloria is going to need a bigger pan!!"

After nearly joining his quarry in the dark waters of the lake he managed to compose himself. Slowly, slowly, he began to reel in his line, every few minutes pausing while he caught his breath at which point his protagonist took advantage and reeled back a bit.

"Oh Gawd," he thought. "This could take some time."

He was beginning to have desperate thoughts of, having hooked his biggest ever fish, but not being able to land it. He could just imagine trying to explain it to Denis, and Denis's sarcastic response,

"Yeh sure Eddie, a really big one eh?"

And Gloria's, "I really don't know why you bother Eddie."

But progress was being made and after what seemed like an eternity his spirits rose somewhat when twenty metres from the shore, he could see, a definite disturbance on the surface of the water which soon became the distinct thrashing of a sizeable fish. By this time his excited screams and hollers had attracted the notice of the other fishermen whose attentions had turned from the incandescent rages of Marcel to the frustrated outpourings of, 'ze simpleton'.

"Zut alors! Ze filet, ze gaf. Vite! Vite!"

Immediately several nets and gaffs were thrust towards Eddie, it was his fish, and it was his, 'honneur', he must land the monster himself.

With shouts of encouragement from his new band of brothers, Eddie summoned up all of his remaining energy. He would show Denis, he would show Gloria. They would never again smirk at Eddie's fishing prowess. Buoyed up by the noise of the crowd, adrenalin coursing through his veins, he dragged and he dragged. The monster was getting closer and closer to the shore, its huge fins were mostly out of the water, its huge mouth gaping and gasping, its huge tail thrashing and those dark, dark, empty, soulless, eyes staring at nothing, closer, closer, closer, when suddenly………. ……………. urged on by a chorus of noisy cheers, and with one last huge effort, Eddie managed to drag the struggling monster out of the lake and onto the shore.

All 23 pounds of it! Another massive cheer went up which echoed around the vast volcanic amphitheatre of the lake.

In his excitement Eddie, rather unnecessarily, swung the gaff, clumsily managing to catch the fish in such a way that ensured that it wouldn't be returning to the lake any time soon. And there, despite the significant facial injury inflicted by Eddie, it lay in all its magnificence, Twenty-three pounds of muscle and sinew. Still twitching ever so slightly, as the last remnants of electrical nerve energy drained from its mighty frame, nearly two metres in length.

"Un grand ZANDER!!! MAGNIFIQUE!!!" announced Monsieur Mureau, "Magnifique!"

The surrounding fishermen stared in wonder, any lingering feelings of envy snuffed out by a sense of awe and admiration. Who was this simpleton? Where was he from? How come no one recognised him?

Eddie just stood there grinning.

Marcel having recovered his wit enough to realise that pursuing Denis wearing his waders was not going to work, had returned to his vehicle just in time to hear the hysterical cheering which could only mean one thing. His humiliation complete, he was now scouring the country lanes in his battered van and, if it were possible, even more determined to kill the English cretin.

❖ ❖ ❖

Denis and his party had, at last, managed to locate the water resort at the other end of the lake and were enjoying the sun-bathing and water slides in equal measure. At least his companions were. Denis was still pondering that they had at some point to return to pick up Eddie so it wasn't with quite the same gay abandon that he plunged into the waters to cool off, in more ways than one. After diving deep into the surprisingly cold lake Denis, generally being a glass-half-full man, surfaced feeling that most of his troubles had been magically washed away, at least for now. Anyway, what was the worst that the mad French man with the bulging eyes and the massive muscles could do?

"Hm, time for another plunge." he thought.

Denis, the romantic, loved nothing better than freshwater swimming. To him, it just seemed such a natural way to embrace nature in all its rawness. Sometimes however the willingness of Denis's spirit could be over-ruled by the weakness of his flesh and on this occasion, it was the temperature of the water that was taking his breath away rather than the nature surrounding it.

For a while he swam around, marvelling at the beauty of the scenery encircling the lake, and the wilderness stretching out endlessly just beyond the little enclave of the leisure park. The top few inches of the water were quite warm but it quickly went very cold not far from the surface interfering with his body's ability to adjust to the temperature.

After a while, he had had enough of embracing nature and headed over to Jack and Clare who were in the process of trying to drown each other but as soon as they were joined by their dad they immediately ganged up on him instead. It wasn't long before he realised that he was never going to win a game of who can drown who first with Clare and Jack and decided that it was time to leave them to it, and joined the gals on the beach.

Maisie and Gloria still oblivious to what had prompted Denis's strange behaviour in the car park earlier that day were cooking nicely in the afternoon sunshine. Maisie had decided that any explanation would probably only spoil an otherwise very pleasant, if somewhat delayed, afternoon of sun-worshipping. Gloria, apart from almost drowning in a sea of mud, had soon forgotten most of the morning's goings-on, anyway, being on holiday with the Wilsons was never going to be boring.

The resort of the Cournon d'Auvergne, was a veritable oasis of civilized calm and peace after the events of the morning, well give or take the hysterical screams and laughter of hundreds of kids enjoying the water slides and rides. Clare and Jack who when it came to days out, had long since accepted the inevitable gap between departure and arrival were happy now that they had finally arrived. Clare though, throughout the dramas of the morning, had had her usual moments of, 'quiet desperation'.

Though somewhat curtailed, the amount of time that they had at the resort was just sufficient and by the time Clare and Jack had satisfied their appetites for thrills on the water slides and Maisie and Gloria were 'cooked' on both sides, they were all happy to call it a day. Anyway they were all beginning to feel a little peckish and as Gloria had rather sarcastically reminded them it was, courtesy of Eddie.

"Fish and chips for tea!!" Ho ho.

Denis, though a little less eager to leave, realised that he had at some point to bite the proverbial bullet and head back in the direction of Eddie, hopefully without bumping into the guy with the maniacal eyes on the way. Summoning up as much enthusiasm as he could, he announced,

"Come on then, let's see what Eddie has caught for our tea!"

Marcel was a veteran of pursuit. Fishing was his pastime, hunting was his passion. His prey was usually wild boar which when he was not fishing he would track relentlessly throughout the forests and hills of his beloved Regional Du Livradois Forez. He knew every inch of the area. The wild boar was a canny old adversary. Dangerous when roused, tireless and smart, vicious when cornered. Marcel had had many an epic battle against the king of the forest and carried many scars to remind him of the dangers of underestimating this particular foe. But today's challenge was different. He knew that he would soon sniff out this 'idiot' and when he caught him he would take great pleasure in disassembling him limb from limb (ooer!). He knew because there was only one place a camper load of foreigners would be heading, le plan d'eau loisir at the other end of the lake! He headed straight there and parked up just outside the only exit, and then, just as when pursuing his favourite prey, he hunkered down and waited for it to appear.

Unfortunately for Marcel, he hadn't allowed for Denis's occasional lapses in concentration.

Exiting the carpark, Denis neglected to pay attention to the sign saying, 'EXIT' and left through the 'ENTRANCE' gate.

"Where the hell are you going Jaques?" screamed Denis at the bemused driver heading straight for him.

"You're driving out through the entrance Denis!" Maisie screamed hysterically, as he swerved just in time to avoid a collision with the shocked driver just coming in.

"Oh for goodness sake Maisie, calm down will you." he shouted above the screams in the back. "Blimey, I broke a rule in France. It's hardly likely to change the course of my life."

"Well it nearly did, idiot!" replied Maisie with uncanny prescience. If only she knew!

By the time Marcel the thug had spotted some distance away, the unmistakable English vehicle leaving the car-park entrance, Denis was already scuttling off down the country lanes oblivious to the attention of his pursuer. In the meantime, two more cars had exited the park and were between him and Denis who by now was already some way ahead. Slamming his van into gear he pressed the pedal to the metal and with a boom of black smoke headed off in pursuit. Denis relying solely on his ability to simply retrace his steps, was already a little confused as each hedgerow looked much like the last and each junction remarkably similar too.

"Do you know where you're going Denis?" enquired Maisie rhetorically.

"Yes of course! ….No not really." he muttered under his breath.

Though Eddie the navigator, as Denis called his friend with a certain dose of irony, was not a huge help when they were trying to find their way somewhere he was at least company and added moral support when the ladies in the back began to get restless. Sadly today, in the absence of his friend, Denis was truly alone. And being alone he adopted his fallback method of getting from A to B, the maze method.

Denis surmised that if when arriving at a junction he alternated turning right and then left, the elementary laws of logic would at some point deliver them to the right place. This theory though a little tenuous did at least provide a strategy which was better than wandering around aimlessly, well slightly better, and it did, when interrogated by his wife, enable him to respond with a certain confidence that at least he knew what he was doing, if not where he was going. Remarkably, unbeknown to Denis, what it did result in was that he and his passengers were becoming more and more mired in the veritable maze of country lanes and that by this time Marcel the thug had totally lost them. Marcel could not believe the guile of his quarry, he had underestimated his prey. His fury was reaching boiling point, defeat staring him in the face when around the corner came Denis. Left and then right and then left and then right and…….. heading unmistakably to the fishing meet.

"Bingo! Idiot!" Marcel smiled triumphantly.

Screeching like a lunatic Marcel took off in pursuit.

By this time Denis was gently bathing in illusions that as it had been a long time ago since he had shouted insults at the nutter in the van he had probably forgotten all about it, hadn't he?

Alerted by the sound of screeching, Denis glanced in the mirror and caught site of the angry lunatic, who he had earlier shouted "asshole" at, looking extremely angry and bearing down on him!

"Oh Gawd! Obviously not." he thought.

◆ ◆ ◆

Back at the lake shore the prize giving ceremony had begun and the beaming Monsieur Mureau was busy presenting the prizes.

The heaviest trout, the most trout caught, the longest trout, the largest catfish, the most fish caught overall, the novice's prize, the veteran's prize, the prize for participating prize and on it went until finally and after a suitably long speech the moment that they had all been waiting for.

With some ceremony, a huge trophy was carried out and placed on a table covered with a white cloth. Then, to much applause, the hero of the day, Eddie, was ushered up onto the podium followed by various local dignitaries who in keeping with the tradition of the annual competition were called forward to receive their award.

The local mayor received his slice of fish, for which he thanked the Chief Marshall. Then le President of the local fishing association another slice, the Park Ranger received a big piece and was also thanked for his continued monitoring of the lake's water quality, to which he responded by making a speech which went on a bit and was unceremoniously brought to a close through various coughs and rude comments from the crowd.

Finally, amidst gestures of feigned embarrassment, Chief Marshall Monsieur Mureau himself was called forward to receive a very generous portion. Eddie, who had not seen his monster fish since just after it had been officially weighed, was already a little confused but now began to get increasingly edgy as he realised that the fish being presented looked remarkably like his zander. When the last huge piece had appeared carrying the unmistakable signs of his clumsy blow with the gaff, he was becoming more than agitated, he was getting angry. At that point, Eddie was called to the centre of the stage and with more words of congratulations Monsieur Mureau presented him with a huge Trophy and to even louder cheers,

"Le grand prize! La tete!"

There on a silver platter staring up at him with those cold, cold eyes, was the massive head of Eddie's zander.

Realising that his worst fears were indeed correct, Eddie the navigator, usually mild and unruffled was about to kick off.

"Where's my fish?" he shouted to the shock of the crowd. "Where's me bloody fish?!"

Picking up the fish head, a raging Eddie shouted, "You can keep your bloody 'tet'!" And flung the thing across the dais hitting Monsieur Mureau full in the side of the head and off the platform where he did an impressive, if somewhat impromptu crowd-surf, before hitting the ground.

By now the 'mutterings' on the podium and in the crowd had risen to shouts of shock and incredulity. This could not be tolerated, "Monsieur Mureau! Zut alors!"
To a man, the outraged crowd surged forward intent on avenging the dishonour of their esteemed Chief Marshall. The whole podium began to rock and shake under the pressure and Eddie was beginning to fear for his life.

At that point Denis came screeching around the bend followed by the mad axeman Marcel. In an instant, the heads of the whole crowd swivelled 90 degrees.

"IN!!" he screamed, throwing open the passenger door. "IN!!!!"

"Les Anglais, les Anglais!!!!" they shouted.

Eddie grabbed his trophy and jumped off the stage and into the camper pausing momentarily to scream back at the raging mob,

"You've nicked me zander you bastards!!! You French bloody bastards!!"

The crowd realising that, as well as the outrageous abuse heaped upon their prestigious annual event, they had been hoodwinked by an imposter, moved towards the camper in a vain attempt at pursuit but Denis was gone and they only succeeded in blocking the progress of a battered Renault 4 van and its blazing passenger.

Denis never looked back until he was well away from the scene. The passengers, themselves in a state of shock and confusion, sat open-mouthed as the drama unfolded. They had seen the genuine fury in the faces of the men storming towards the camper as Denis had blazed away. They didn't know what had caused their anger but it hadn't looked good. And they knew it had been a close shave.

After a few miles, a silence descended. Maisie sat behind Denis, staring at him. He knew she was because he could feel the heat of her glare, imprinting, "I want an explanation." on the back of his head.

Gloria had recovered enough to draw a positive from the whole terrifying drama,

"Wow you've won a prize Eddie!" she said, staring at the trophy and pretending that she had just noticed it.

Eddie's mood lightened and his pride swelled ever so slightly.

"It's massive. Where's the fish?" she continued still confused. Nice one Gloria!

Eddie, a mix of immense pride and seething anger, held on to his trophy like it was his little child.

That evening back in the relative safety of the campsite the mood was quiet. But glancing over at Eddie, Denis couldn't help a wry smile. Eddie was sitting clutching onto his prize and gently polishing it with a piece of old dishcloth.

"Bloomin' shame." thought Denis. "First time I've known him to catch a fish. And it must have been a bloody big one too."

They had all listened fascinated to Eddie's tale of woe, which Gloria kept interrupting with irritating questions, that culminated in,

"So what happened to the fish then?"

She didn't get the ancient tradition bit.

Denis had filled in the other pieces in the jigsaw of events but it didn't seem to assuage Maisie's vexation. When they all finally turned in, Denis lay in bed staring at the canvass ceiling reflecting on how the hell once again he got to be blamed when things had gone ever so slightly wrong. Finally, he drifted off and silence descended onto the campsite.

The first disturbance was at about 01am. A hideous scream came from the tent next door.

"What the hell….?"

"Gloria's found the fish head." mused Denis. "I did warn him not to put it in the nighttime portaloo. Why would you do that?"

After Gloria's disturbing interruption, sleep was evading Denis. Every time he heard the sound of a car his body went rigid as he considered the possibility of the mad French man tracking them down and murdering him in his sleep. Next to him his faithful, if somewhat immutable wife sensed his discomfort. She also reflected on whether maybe she had been a little harsh on her poor husband. It had been difficult negotiating their way around the myriad of French country lanes and Eddie was not much help. But he should have bought a decent map. And that Frenchman's reaction had been a bit OTT, she had never seen such angry eyes. But then Denis shouldn't have called him what he did. But he did get them to the park eventually and it had been a lovely afternoon. And if stupid Gloria hadn't decided to wash her legs in the lake and if she hadn't dropped her bloomin' soap dish. After all, it had been Denis who had rescued her even if he had uprooted a sapling in a National Park to do it. And he had rescued them twice from the mad French bloke. And the way he managed to evade him all the way from the lake to the bit where they were fishing had been uncanny. Poor Denis she leaned over to give him a hug but hesitated when she heard, ZZzzzzzz ZZzzzzzz.

It was about four in the morning, the most vulnerable hour, apparently, when Denis heard the vehicle arrive. He heard the unmistakable sound of a door opening and quietly closing. The soft pad of footsteps approaching the tent. Suddenly the whole interior lit up. Silhouetted like a projection on a screen, a huge figure was illuminated at the end of the bed. Denis stared in horror as a horrible searing noise ripped through the thin canvass, standing before him was Marcel his eyes ablaze, in his right hand a huge axe dripping with blood.

"AAAHHHHHHHH!!!!!!!!!!!!!!" screamed Denis

"AHHHH!!!!" screamed Maisie "What the hell Denis? DENIS! Wake Up!!"

◆ ◆ ◆

It was a cool night out at the lake, a night of sepulchral silence before it was disturbed by the strange scream somewhere in the distance, which for a few seconds echoed around the dark hills before being swallowed up by the enveloping peace.

Mr and Mrs Slovenian grebe had just arrived and looked at each other quizzically before settling down again for a well-earned rest. They would have arrived a week earlier had it not been for some rather unseasonable weather over the Alps, but at last they were here, back in their favourite winter resting grounds.

"Goodness only knows what that screaming was." remarked Mr Slovenian grebe.

"Yes strange. But isn't it nice to be back?" replied Mrs Slovenian grebe.

"Shame we're late. It is such a place of peace and solitude. And I do miss being greeted by those funny men with trees on their heads."

◆ ◆ ◆

As Denis drifted deeper into his snowy tomb his memories also drifted further back into the past. In fact right to the very beginning......

CHAPTER 4

It was a very quiet morning when Denis rose early from his rather narrow bed. His excitement tempered with a little trepidation, the adventure was beginning today and apart from the frequent trips to Bridlington in the East, and Southport to the West, the furthest he had previously travelled from his humble abode had been to the distant realms of, wait for it…… Ilfracombe, North Devon! And boy that had been some adventure. Denis had been ten at the time and was, of course, in the company of his parents.

Today was different. Today the world beckoned, well at least France. He could hardly contain his excitement and would love to have shared it with his parents, but unfortunately they had both already left for work.

French France, abroad, where they speak a different language, ate different food, where it was always hot and you could, on no account, drink the water. And after France, who knows? Germany, that couldn't be far away. Holland? Belgium? Italy? Greece? Turkey? Israel on one of those, 'Kibbutz' things that he had read about somewhere. Apparently, you could volunteer and live there for ages eating oranges, which one of his primary school teachers had once told the class, grew in people's gardens!! But anyway that was for the future, today was France and he was ready.

It was a gap year but long before, to Denis's knowledge, gap years had even been invented. Never one to dance to other people's tunes, Denis had not excelled in his years of formal education, his claim to fame being that he was one of the few boys not to be appointed as a school prefect, a distinction for which he felt a quiet sense of pride.

Now he was free of all that, his life before him, and enough money saved over the period since finishing his 'A' levels from his employment working for a painting contractor, to catapult him across the channel, via the train from London Victoria to Dover and from there to Calais France, Europe, the World, the Universe and beyond!! It was September 1973. Denis was…. 'just seventeen, well you know what I mean?...' Actually he was eighteen, but don't spoil it.

He had called in the shop to say goodbye to his rather distraught mother, who along with a whole generation who had survived the war, was still getting used to her son being a 'teenager', a phenomenon that had also only recently been invented. Being a teenager included wearing weird clothes, listening to weird music, growing weirdly long hair, and generally weird behaviour, including weird ideas like travelling abroad with no apparent acknowledgement of the future and the need to prepare for it.

In the past, the only reason most English people had gone to France, was to fight!

"There's a whole crowd of us." he reassured his parents when he had informed them of his intention of going travelling for a year before deciding on his future.

"You know Des? His Mum is all right with it."

Denis's Dad, an unassuming humble soul, who had been through his own European adventure less than thirty years earlier, didn't have the energy to argue and just 'kept his head down'. He had, along with his comrades, developed a level of stoicism which had helped him survive.

He had picked up one French phrase during his own ordeal, 'sanfairyann', a kind of equivalent of the modern-day, 'it is what it is'. He had been told repeatedly by his comrades in arms, sanfairyann.

'It doesn't matter.'

"Just avoid Normandy." he told Denis, "Their beaches are a nightmare!"

With this curious warning, which Denis didn't fully understand, rolling around his head, he bade his parents farewell, and leaving behind all the comforts of domesticity, caught the number 40 bus into town, before boarding the London-bound coach. The 'whole crowd' of enthusiastic companions accompanying him on this adventure, had by now dwindled to just two intrepid souls, Des and Paul.

Denis's Mum, because she was Denis's Mum, had packed him some Marks & Spencer's potted meat sandwiches for the journey, which were, initially scoffed by Des and Paul, meaning rejected not eaten. However, they later changed their minds on that one. Oh yes.

Even before they had reached embarkation day, for this particular band of brothers, things had not gone too well. They knew that they needed tents, as they would be camping in fields and things, and so they had purchased two very good, sturdy specimens, both two-man. Being of good quality, the tents along with sleeping bags and their initial transport costs, had already eaten into their limited budget. Unfortunately, the tents did not come with ground sheets, a fact that they had discovered when, prior to the departure date, in order to make sure they knew how to put them up, they had constructed one of them in Des's garden. A missing groundsheet seemed a minor matter at the time. Oh dear.

Unfortunately the next morning, the missing groundsheet was indeed a minor matter. Having left the erected tent in Des's back garden overnight, the next morning it had gone! Nicked!!

Denis never did quite recover from this shock, and forever after struggled when it came to anything to do with the construction of tents. As many years later, his future wife Maisie would testify.

"Oh crap!" was the general reaction. Unfortunately, buying another tent was out of the question.

"Well, three of you in a two-man tent, with all your bags. At least you will be warmer." suggested Des's Mum helpfully.

Equipped therefore with two haversacks, one tent, a sleeping bag each, 'some' clothes and quite randomly, in Denis's bag, a portable tape recorder and some music tapes, they arrived some hours later in London, having relatively smoothly, successfully completed phase one of the great adventure that would take them around Europe and onto that 'Kibbutz thing'. For some strange reason, Paul had chosen to bring something resembling a Gladstone bag with him, it was as if he hadn't planned to stay.

With their long hair and denim fatigues, they understandably stood out from the usual train passengers, but as they settled into the journey from London to Dover, they were all feeling quite perky. And apart from the minor disturbance caused by getting their bags and tent through the train's narrow door, and then locating vacant seats on the rather busy route, they blended in fairly well with the other travellers on board. The major problem had been Denis and his haversack. Built for bulk rather than slenderness, it was slightly wider than Denis, so as he squeezed along the aisle in the carriage looking for a spare seat, he managed to clobber a number of passengers in the head as he passed by. Unfortunately, it was a while before he realised that the resultant indignant voices behind were actually directed at him. His loyal companions were enjoying it too much to tell him, so by the time he had found a vacant seat he had already set himself apart. Still, things soon settled down, but unfortunately, it would not be the last time that his oversized haversack would cause consternation in the narrow spaces of public transport.

The feeling of contentment at having completed phase one of the journey, i.e. catching the train, did not however last long. Though Paul's Gladstone bag, the subject of previous ribaldry, had slipped comfortably into the overhead luggage space, the clumsy haversacks, having been spotted by an overzealous 'jobsworth', were now sitting in the baggage car. Prompted by the image of the empty lawn, where the tent had previously resided fresh in their memories, whilst Paul slept, Denis and Des had taken it in turns to sit with them. It wasn't quite the romantic picture, the ever-romantic Denis had carried in his mind for the last few weeks, but as he kept telling himself, it was all part of the adventure.

Fortunately, the journey to Dover was less than two hours, and as it was a ferry train, it unloaded its passengers pretty much onto the ferry boat, which wasted no time in leaving for its 90-minute voyage to Calais. Denis found it surprising that the passage was so short, he had always imagined that going abroad involved a very long journey across the sea. But they were soon walking down the exit ramp and onto French soil, or at least French tarmac. Denis experienced a frisson of excitement as his feet hit terra firma. Here he was abroad, in a foreign country. It was an excitement which trailed rather quickly as the boys reached les douaniers and passport control.

By now it was already late afternoon, whilst their boat had

still been mid-channel the sun had disappeared below the horizon and now it was rapidly becoming dark. They had been somewhat thrown by the amount of ticket checking through which they had already been subjected to, buses, trains and boats and now passports. It was for all of them, apart from Paul who had once been on a school trip to St. Malo, the first time they had been on a trip of such variety and had usually been accompanied by their parents, and therefore never before had to worry about paperwork. What neither helped was that the officials who checked their tickets were not always sympathetic, and often quite brusque. The French passport controllers added another element of difficulty by, surprisingly, speaking French.

The sum total of Denis's French was what he had managed to gain despite seven years of school lessons. Seven years may sound like a decent apprenticeship and it had ensured Denis a GCE, but when Denis had hoped to extend his language skills by studying French at A level in the Sixth Form, he had had to endure two years of the existential works of Jean-Paul Sartre and Albert Camus! A course of study which had involved no conversational skills. Denis would always maintain that Satre's, 'Les Jeux Sont Faits' not only messed with his head but ruined his blossoming mastery of French.

Still, he wasn't bitter, much.

Though desperate to try out his skills, being confronted with an even less than sympathetic official, he realised that his schoolboy French wasn't worth employing. He just stood passively handing over his passport and saying, 'oui' or 'non', whenever it seemed appropriate.

Due to the time taken to pass through the various checks, it meant that by now it was well and truly dark. They were also well and truly exhausted, and well and truly starving. The rigours of negotiating passport control had somewhat dampened their excitement so that by now, even the usually indomitable Denis was beginning to wane. The further realisation that French life, in terms of places to purchase any type of food, had long since closed up for the night really did sink their collective spirits further. That was until Denis remembered that squashed all day somewhere deep in his haversack, lurked his mother's Marks & Spencer's potted beef sandwiches, which his previously sceptical companions wasted no time in helping him devour.

"Was it really only that same morning that she had made them?" mused Denis.

It had been a long day!

Denis's parents may have been a little concerned about their son's lack of plans for the future, but they would have been even more concerned had they realised the paucity of his plans for this, present great European adventure. Though at some point, the companions having realised, or at least having been advised, that they would need to take French money with them, had actually changed some of their cash into Francs, they then, based on very little logic, decided that the rest would be changed into Deutsch Marks. Denis with his 'O' level in economics had heard that it was a particularly strong currency.

Sadly, apart from managing to acquire the French francs, questions like where they would spend the first night was something they had not really addressed. Probably in a field. They did after all have their tents, albeit now, a tent. It was therefore more luck than judgement that they stumbled across that welcome French facility, the municipal campsite, which though not too far from the port, did involve a walk.

Not long after leaving the environs of the port, they saw and followed the sign, 'Municipal Camping', and not long after that, arrived at what amounted to little more than a field with a toilet block. Being late September, the field was understandably empty and so they had full use of the real estate stretching out before them, and after some discussion, decided to pitch close to, but having seen the very French toilets, not too close to, the toilet block. With the benefit of the rehearsal in Des's back garden, it didn't take very long to pitch camp and they found that even with their haversacks and Paul's Gladstone, the space inside the tent was quite adequate. It also ensured that there would be no falling out over who would get a tent to themselves.

Responding to the sudden dip in temperature, they wasted no time in getting, fully clothed, into their sleeping bags, and it wasn't long before the absence of a groundsheet began to bite.

"The first day." Denis thought, "French France! WOW!"

And then not much else.

The next day, true to form and belying the fact that he was a teenager, Denis was up at first light and already embracing his new surroundings. His sleepy companions would not be the first ones to mutter incredulity,

"For goodness sake Denis! What time is it?" groaned Paul.

In future years it might be the rising heat of the tent which would rouse him, but on this occasion, it was the night spent in a sense of encroaching hypothermia which had forced him up. Des and Paul, though sharing a similar night of discomfort, did not have Denis's resolve. Their two embryonic forms were still buried deep in their sleeping bags and clinging onto the forlorn hope that things might improve. Not to be, I'm afraid.

At least life was slowly seeping back into Denis's body. The lack of a groundsheet, a must for insulation, and sleeping bags more designed for indoor use, had contributed little to a night of peaceful slumber but resulted rather in severe distress. It was going to be a steep learning curve.

By the time the others had managed to drag themselves up, the sun was beginning to have some influence on the temperature of this field in Northern France, and Denis who had already discovered the parlous state of the ablutions was rather annoyingly already back on speed. Not literally of course.

Mixing up some of the few bits of things he remembered learning from his GCE History, he threw his arms wide and as if announcing to the rest of France, proceeded to regale his companions with….

"Quick quick boys, an ecstasy of fumbling on this St Crispin's Day, we happy band of brothers, in England now a-bed shall think themselves accursed they were not here!"

"For in some foreign field will be forever England."

"Dulce et decorum est pro patria mori."

"YES!!"

By the time he had finished his rousing call to arms, his companions had already disappeared into the toilet block to escape.

As soon as the happy band had regrouped, their thoughts turned to breakfast, another thing which they had imagined would just happen. It usually did at home. Curiously, although Denis had packed the tape recorder and music tapes, cooking equipment was not on their list of necessary items to bring. Still, they had money and there were shops surely not too far away because they had passed them last night in the dark. Denis, armed with his GCE French, was dispatched as hunter-gatherer while Des and Paul luxuriated in the September sunshine which by now was beginning to really warm up.

It wasn't long before he came across a boulangerie. Denis strode in confidently and was immediately struck by the delicious odour hitting his nostrils. Quickly recovering his composure, and in his perfect schoolboy French, he asked for a loaf.

"Er, pain s'il vous plait."

"Oui, lequel monsieur?" responded the young lady, signalling to a whole range of breads from, baguettes, to ficelle, to pain de campagne, to boulle de pain and on and on and all stacked up behind her.

Not quite sure what she meant, Denis hesitated,

"Erm,er.."

"Un baguette?" she responded helpfully.

"Ah oui merci, un baguette." of course, he recognised that from way back.

Now on a roll, Denis continued.

"Lait." he said.

"Lait?"

"Er, lait, er milk?" he stuttered.

"Lait!" next door she replied pointing, and seeming to imply, "Milk here? This is a boulangerie, you idiot!"

"Ah oui, merci."

Denis having no idea what he was being asked for in payment, proffered a 100 franc note, about ten pounds, which the young lady, despite being rather taken aback, received with grace, and with a big smile, gave Denis his large amount of change.

Next door at the épicerie the items were rather more accessible and so other than voicing a very clear, "Bonjour." as he entered, he was able to reserve the rest of his French for another day.

"Bonjour monsieur." responded the welcoming gentleman on the other side of the door.

Helping himself to a bottle of milk, he spied what appeared to be a rather nice piece of cheese which he thought would go down well back at the camp. It turned out to be butter.

Denis, extremely happy with his shopping trip, and of course his GCE French, munched contentedly on the results of his labours and returned to the campsite with a definite spring in his step.

As the boys tucked into their buttered baguettes, which after the initial disappointment of discovering it wasn't cheese, hadn't really mattered, Denis reflected on his first encounter with French France. He had loved it.

"Where now brave fellows, where now? Europe is awaiting!"

After some discussion about where to go next and not getting much further than, "Paris is in France." The boys were at a bit of an impasse until Paul quite casually disclosed that his mother had packed him a map,

"Oh yeh." he said, "I had forgotten."

Unfortunately in response to his declaring to his parents, "I'm off round Europe." It was a map of Europe rather than France, so lacked a bit of detail, actually quite a lot, and also later was to distract the boys from exploring France a little longer. Never staying very long in one place was to become an unfortunate theme of the trip. Being naive in their travelling, they failed to see that towns abroad were just like English towns, they were towns, they needed time and exploration to reveal their secrets and delights. As soon as they had arrived in a place and found nothing of immediate attraction, they moved on.

Thus, after quickly striking camp, which given the amount of camp to strike, did not take long, Calais was dismissed with barely a glance, and managing to hitch a lift on the back of a farmer's trailer full of turnips, they were soon speeding off to Dunkirk, which they had all heard of and reckoned would be far more interesting.

Whilst taking care to avoid the odd errant turnip, the impact of which, as Des had discovered early into the journey, if travelling at speed could really hurt, the boys settled down and were feeling upbeat, though as the benefits of the bread and butter breakfast wore off, a little hungry. Actually, 'speeding along' in a tractor-trailer full of turnips was not quite how it was and so the twenty-five-mile journey to Dunkirk took somewhat longer than they had anticipated.

By the time they arrived, it was already late afternoon and after first buying some cooked meat and cheese from a little mini-market, they set off exploring the town, which they were vaguely aware had been the scene of an evacuation sometime during the second world war. Sadly it didn't take them that long. French towns and villages generally can be very quiet places once noon hour has passed and never really get going again until later in the evening. At five o'clock at night, they are positively sepulchral. This prompted Denis to irreverently observe,

"I can understand why the Brits wanted to get out so fast."

They were struggling to decide what they would do next when they heard voices that sounded familiar.

"Hey they're Americans." said Paul pointing towards a bunch of similarly aged young men standing next to a Transit van near the quayside. The young Americans at the same time spotted the boys and they all strolled over to each other.

"Where you heading?" asked one.

"Not sure really. We only arrived yesterday and we are still getting organised." replied Des.

"And you?"

"Well we've just arrived from the UK with this old Transit and we're planning to kit it out at some point to do some travelling. We're heading off for Paris tonight."

"Wanna come?" said another.

Looking at each other without speaking but with a mix of surprise and hesitancy, the boys were all clearly thinking the same thing. That they really had had enough of Dunkirk, and that the idea of getting a ride straight to Paris? Well it was a bit of a no-brainer.

"It's a bit rough in there." they were warned. "There aren't any seats, just a couple of foamies but not much else."

"Yeh that's great." said Denis quickly, as he noticed Paul frowning ever so slightly.

"Great, thanks a lot."

Piling into the Ford Transit, the boys were accompanied in the back by a couple of the Americans who generously shared the 'foamies' with their new buddies.

"So how long will it take to get there?" asked Des, ever the practical one.

"Oh, good question." answered the driver. "Well it's about 200 miles, so in this thing, about five hours."

"Five hours! Oh right, yeh of course." replied Des.

The boys stared at each other, individually computing the implications of arriving in Paris well after midnight and also understood the reason for the foam mattresses.

It didn't take much conversation before they discovered that the Americans were actually Canadians from Montreal. It was when two of the boys frequently slipped into what Denis realised was French that their curiosity had been raised, and when quizzed, the boys explained about Quebec and French Canada.

"Blimey, I never realised." said Denis. "People in Canada speak French!"

There was a noticeable chuckle at Denis's, "blimey"

"Yeh we're all from around Montreal, well Clarence is from closer to Ottawa."

"That's right, my folks are Native Indian, from the Algonquin peoples around Augusta."

Denis had noticed earlier that Clarence appeared to have slightly bronzed skin and wondered if he might be Asian.

"Indians in Canada! Wow!" he thought, "I thought Indians were from America."

The conversation flowed easily. The boys were all of a similar age, and the Canadians had that relaxed affable Canadian way about them. They traded stories about their respective homelands, their motivation for travelling and their plans for the trip. One of the boys happened to mention that they might end up going south to do some grape picking. At one point the English boys were taken aback to discover that their fellow travellers frequently smoked 'weed', as they called it, as it was quite common in Canada and obviously not such a 'no no' there. Things were different in France so they hadn't brought any with them.

"Shame." thought Des.

"Thank God." thought Denis.

But Denis's mind was still occupied with the mention of grape picking. Quizzing them further it emerged that it was something very much part of the scene further south. Especially around Bordeaux, grape producers were desperate for reliable pickers to get in the harvest as soon as it was ready. It was generally well paid and also provided food and accommodation but you had to commit to completing the harvest once you'd started.

"Wow sounds great!" thought Denis. And the others agreed.

After a while, the party settled down and tried to sleep away the rest of the journey. Paul managed to stretch himself out using his Gladstone bag as a pillow and slept. Denis tried to do likewise with his haversack but it didn't quite work the same. Des just sat up and leaned against the inner panel of the van, his head comically banging against the side every time they went over a bit of a bump.

"Where there's no sense...." chuckled Denis, as he drifted off to sleep.

The journey was just shy of five hours and ended in a lay-by slightly outside the centre of Paris. It was 1 a.m.

"Well this is it guys." announced the driver. "Not much doing now until morning, so get comfy."

Setting their seats back, the driver and the front passenger stayed where they were which meant it allowed the others to, as best they could, share the bits of foam. Sadly at some point, Denis had slipped off his little bit of mattress and spent the night on the floor. If he thought sleeping in a tent without a ground sheet was bad he had never imagined trying to sleep on the freezing metal surface of a van. It was excruciatingly cold.

Waking up seriously shivering, it didn't help after several hours of punctuated sleep, to see Paul still completely stretched out on a foam mattress and apparently in deep slumber. Poor Des, obviously missing the memo, was still leaning against the side of the van, though he had at some point managed to get into his sleeping bag.

Dropping them off at the crack of dawn, right in the centre, there were lots of grateful handshakes and genuine goodbyes as the two groups went their separate ways. The Canadians heading to somewhere outside Paris where they had a contact who would help them work on the van and the English boys to explore gay Paris. No not that kind of 'gay' this was 1973!

"You take care guys and have blimey good travels." quipped Clarence.

They all laughed but at the same time, it was all quite sad, as a definite bond had begun to form.

They wouldn't even accept any contribution for petrol.

"No look we were coming here anyway, maybe next time."

It was the end of chapter one.
Well here they were, Paris, France after having left home just two days earlier.

It wasn't until their friends had departed that on turning around they realised that they were actually in spitting distance of the Arc de Triomphe, one of Paris's most iconic buildings.

 Constructed around 1833, after being commissioned in 1806 to celebrate Emperor Napoleon's victory at Austerlitz, it is, along with the Eiffel Tower, one of Paris's most recognisable features. For the young boys who had travelled little and had only encountered the world's most famous edifices either in books or occasionally on TV, this was amazing. For Denis it was spellbinding.

They all stood and stared not quite believing what they could see. But before exploring further the only things on their minds just now were breakfast and toilets and they wasted no time in disappearing into the nearest café.

Even by fellow French people, Parisians can be considered somewhat haughty and aloof. To the boys, cafés were where you had a cup of tea and maybe a sandwich or pie. So inevitably as they fell into a rather pristinely appointed establishment somewhere adjoining the Arc de Triomphe, something was bound to give.

Whereas in more modern times when gap years are a compulsory rite of passage, and many young people leaving school do not further their careers until they have travelled the length of South America from Caracas to Tierra del Fuego, boogied on the beaches of Bali, or ridden an elephant in Thailand, in 1973, Denis, Des and Paul were amongst the forerunners of this phenomenon. The patrons of the Paris café scene therefore, not usually seeing tourists outside the tourist season, and certainly not long-haired, haversack-wielding young ones, were a little shocked and bemused when the band of brothers clunked their way into, and across the marble floor of this particular one. Don't make eye contact seemed to be the general agreement of the clientele, but their discreet conversation seemed to have found a common focus; these very strange-looking creatures.

Hubert had witnessed many things in his time as a waiter at the Café Lateral, but never this. However, being a consummate professional, he immediately approached the table occupied by his most recent clients and enquired kindly.

"Oui messieurs?"

Denis was nominated to do the talking, and immediately recognising the waiter's interrogative tone, responded in flawless French.

"Erm, café s'il vous plait."

Just as Hubert was leaving Denis spoilt it somewhat by calling, "Twa.".

His companions looked at him aghast. Hubert immediately spun around and looking Denis straight in the eye said.

"Trois monsieur? Bien sur."

The boys disappeared smirking off into the toilets, leaving Denis wondering what had been so funny. By the time they got back, Denis had also managed to order three croissants.

"Yeh, I remember them from my French lessons." he said sagely.

"Big pastries, the French have them for breakfast." he added, before slipping off for his own ablutions.

By the time he returned his companions were staring at three tiny cups of black coffee and three even tinier pastries. They thought that was bad enough until Hubert brought over the tab!

"Bloody hell!" gasped Denis. (Language Denis!)

If they had been organised enough to have had a daily budget, they had just blown it!

Amidst the stares of the bemused patrons, they clunked their way out of the cafe suitably chastened. And mentally crossing cafés off their places to visit, continued their exploration.

After satisfying their curiosity about the Arc de Triomphe and learning about its role in honouring those who fought in the French Revolutionary and Napoleonic wars, Des and Paul were ready to move on.

"Beneath its vault lies the Tomb of the Unknown Soldier from World War I." read Denis

"Yeh…." he continued. "….we're standing at the western end of the Champs-Élysées at the centre of the Place Charles de Gaulle formally named Place de l'Étoile- the étoile or "star" of the juncture formed by its twelve radiating avenues."

"Fascinating." muttered Paul.

Despite Denis's limited success in his academic pursuits he had a fascination for all things historical and cultural, an interest sadly his companions did not share, and a fact which would begin to frustrate.

So, on discovering that the other major Parisian icon, the Eiffel Tower, was situated only about a mile and a half away on the other side of the River Seine, they made their way there.

Denis, in his tour guide mode, read enthusiastically.

"Constructed in 1889 as the centrepiece of the 1889 world fair, the Eiffel Tower, named after the engineer Gustav Eiffel, was from its construction until 1933, the tallest structure in the world. Nicknamed at the time as the 'Iron Lady' (the original), it was mocked by many leading artists and intellectuals, but now is the most visited monument with an entrance fee in the world, and probably the most recognised."

Again, picture book stuff right in front of them. The boys gawped in awe.

"Wow!" observed Des prosaically. "Is it bigger than the Blackpool Tower?"

"Course, I would think so." answered Denis. "This is Paris."

Discovering that entrance to the tower came at a price, the boys, still smarting from their early morning extravagance, decided against it and anyway the thought of attempting the 1,665 steps from the esplanade to the top, especially with two haversacks and a Gladstone bag, really didn't appeal. Denis would have liked to have at least attempted some of it but felt overruled and just agreed but it was another source of frustration and disappointment.

It was getting way past lunchtime and Paul was grumbling about being starving, which to be fair they all were, but Denis had one more place he wanted to visit, Notre Dame Cathedral. Understandably Des and Paul did not share his interest in visiting a "bloody church", but agreed to at least accompany him to the general area and do some exploring there, arranging to meet up a while later.

It meant an urban bus trip which brought them into conflict with another raft of indignant Parisians. Trying to get onto a crowded bus had been similar to negotiating their way onto the train a few days earlier, with their baggage, not easy. Reactions ranged from irritation to indignation, to downright anger, as, making their way to the back of the bus, particularly Denis, they accidentally knocked into various passengers. After a while, things began to settle. The outraged passengers had managed to exercise most of their indignation, and the relatively short journey was almost complete.

"There it is." spied Denis

That was when Des, inexplicably decided to pull himself up on the two leather ceiling straps that he was holding onto for stability. As he pulled himself up, the bus jerked forward, and Des, suspended in space and hanging like a chimpanzee, swung forward wrapping his legs around a lady in front, before letting go and crashing onto the floor whilst forlornly crying out,

"Sorry! Sorry!"

Well if invading peaceful Parisian cafés on an early September morning had been bad enough the reaction to this was indescribable. To the accompaniment of a cacophony of,

"Ooh la la!"

"Zut alor!" and

"Mon Dieu!"

Our three amigos sensing the uprising of an angry mob had no alternative but to prudently exit the bus at the next stop. With a stream of unintelligible and probably 'colloquial' French directed at them by the driver, ringing in their ears, they tried to look casual as they faced up to the stares of the curious passers-by.

"Welcome to Paris." thought Denis.

As Denis, ever the romantic, stood in the Cathedral of Notre Dame reflecting on the European tour thus far, he couldn't help but begin to entertain heretical thoughts. The crowd of them intending to do the trip in the first place had dwindled down to just him, Des and Paul. Camping had been less than an unqualified success, and he had not slept very well, if at all, since leaving home. After a positive start, the quality of welcome by their hosts had on today's evidence, been less than warm, though there were mitigating circumstances, what the hell was Des doing? But it just wasn't as he had imagined, Paris, France how exciting!

Denis felt very low, and yes a little homesick. In fact a lot. He began to offer up a little prayer and was about to become tearful when the Mass that he had stumbled into suddenly ended and he was carried out on a wave of worshippers exiting the Church. Standing outside waiting for him in the bright sunshine, was Des.

"Right?" he said.

"Me and Paul have been talking and decided that we've probably seen everything in Paris, so why don't we move on. What do you think? Oh and I've got you a sandwich."

Before Denis could answer, Des continued.

"Yeh, there's a station called the gar nord, or something, and we can get a student ticket to Brussels, it's in Belgium, I think. It leaves at 4.30."

Denis buoyed up by Des's enthusiasm and of course, the sandwich, said

"Why not?"

And that is what they did.

The whirlwind nature of the tour was not letting up. Missing their Brussels connection in Charleroi, they decided to bunk down in the station waiting room until the next morning but were soon unceremoniously ejected into the station car park, where they managed to catch a lift in the direction of a campsite with two slightly older girls in a very nice car. The driver, who introduced herself as Anna, Denis always remembered, was curiously bare-footed. Due to some mix-up of language, the girls, despite offering them a bed for the night if all else failed, ended up dropping them at the entrance to the campsite, which, only after the girls had driven away, the boys discovered had been closed for several years and was in fact now a provincial airport, which being late at night was deserted. On the steps of which, they spent their third night abroad.

Managing to catch a bus back to the station early in the morning, they finally managed to complete their journey to Brussels, where having long since abandoned the idea of camping, they wasted no time in locating a hostel. After booking in around four in the afternoon and after finding their respective bunks, Des and Paul immediately took showers and Denis just, 'crashed' and then slept, slept and slept a bit more.

It would have been a bit more as well if they hadn't been woken by a rather strange hostel staff member who seemed to take delight in telling them that it was time to rise and then creepily hanging around. He seemed afterwards to follow Denis down to the showers where he once again, creepily hung around. Des and Paul found it hilarious and could not contain their mirth when Denis shared this piece of information with them.

"Thanks boys." he said.

Breakfast, a simple offering but including an endless supply of bread, jam and bowls of warm coffee, which had never tasted better, was part of the deal, so they at least got off to a good start.

Feeling reinvigorated after a decent sleep in a real bed, and now a more than adequate breakfast, as soon as they had finished they went off to explore. Having spent the night luxuriating in a comfy bed, they unanimously agreed to splash out on a second night, it also meant that they could leave their clumsy bags behind, ensuring that they were locked away.

Belgium, famously famous for not being famous, (a tedious and erroneous description. Ed.), apart from chocolates and being the Germans' favourite route into France, did house something which Denis had read about somewhere, the famous Mannekin Pis, which is Flemish for little pee man. Or in English, a 17th century 24-inch tall bronze statue of a little boy having a pee, which just goes on and on because it also doubles as a fountain. After making enquiries with Marten, the helpful man in reception who told them that it was not far from the Town Hall, which in turn was close to the station where they had landed the previous evening, they set off with various degrees of enthusiasm. Denis was struggling to sell to his companions the cultural aspects of the tour.

As with all directions, so simple to those giving, not so to those receiving, it took much longer to find the little chap than had been anticipated and by the time they got there, doubts were being raised as to why they had spent so much time…

"..searching for some kid having a pee.."

Sadly, the intrinsic value (intrinsic? Is that even a word?) of such a cultural icon, was not shared by Des and Paul. Actually, after struggling through the busy streets of Brussels for over an hour, Denis himself was beginning to harbour his own doubts. Dutifully ticking off the 'Mannekin pis' in his imaginary, I Spy book of things to see in Europe, he stood for a while trying to, 'big it up' but even he had to admit that, OK it was amusing but the two-foot statue before him wasn't the Eiffel Tower or even the Arc de Triomphe.

The hostel, being quite a walk from the station, was situated in a less urban part of the famous city and on the way back they came across a lively market which succeeded in lifting their spirits. They spent ages wandering around the various stands captivated by the range of foodstuffs on offer, some recognisable others not so. The meats, cheeses and pastries seemed to be cascading off the stalls, with one particular one completely covered from tails to trotters, by the parts of several pigs.

"Blimey look at that massive head and it's got its eyes open!" observed Des.

"And look at its blond eyelashes." added Denis.

"Balls." contributed Paul with glee. "Look a huge tray full, over there."

"Uh, how could you eat those!?!"

Being drawn to the lure of a very familiar smell. they moved on,

"Chips!"

"Now you're talking, now you are talking!!" said Paul excitedly.

"How do we say we want some?" asked Des.

"I don't know." replied Denis.

"What do they speak here?" asked Paul, "the bloke in the hostel spoke English and those girls did too."

"I don't actually know. Belgium, and maybe a bit of French I think." Denis answered, a slight feeling of panic in his voice.

"Brilliant!"

But before the panic had taken hold, the helpful lady at the chip van, after relieving them of some money, soon had them holding their own cone-shaped container brimming full of delicious-smelling chips.

"Ask her for some vinegar." urged Paul, I can't see it.

"Er vinegar?" offered Denis not sure what else to say.

"Vinaigre? Mayonnaise." she said pointing to a huge squeezy bottle on the counter.

The boys realising what the other diners were doing, picked it up and warily squirted it onto their chips.

"Hmm." thought Denis, who had hardly even heard of mayonnaise and certainly never put it on his chips!

"It's a bit like salad cream." said Des, "actually, quite good."

By the time they returned to the hostel the boys had decided that they had probably covered most of what Belgium had to offer, i.e. a statue of a peeing boy and oh yes, mayonnaise on chips. In order to continue their forensic tour of Europe therefore, it was probably time to move on. Sitting around the common room table, they poured over Paul's map.

It did not take too much pouring though, because as soon as, and almost at the same time as they spotted Amsterdam, their collective minds were pretty much made up.

"Amsterdam! Now that's supposed to be groovy."

Marten, the kind man at the desk, advised them that rather than taking a train, a far more interesting route was to go by bus to Breskens and take the passenger ferry to Vlissingen. From there they could take a bus to Amsterdam. It would be cheaper and far more scenic than stuck in a crowded train.

"The ferry journey is not too long but can be surprisingly rough, it is late September and it is the North Sea." he added, with a curious wink.

It was indeed a short crossing, though not as short as Paul's map of Europe seemed to suggest, but the 'wink' took on a little more significance as they headed out on the short stretch of sea to Vlissingen.

Standing on opposite sides of the point where the narrow land of the River Scheldt estuary finally widens and releases the river out into the North Sea, the waters seem to compete with each other as to which is coming in and which is going out. The significant turbulence caused by this resulted in the inner decks of the fairly small passenger boat having more in common with the final moments of the Titanic than a quick trip from Belgium to Holland.

"...but can be surprisingly rough," Marten had said. And he wasn't wrong there!

Shaken and a little stirred they couldn't however deny, that it had been, "far more interesting."

It was easy to locate the bus for the three-hour journey to Amsterdam, the main city, and they were soon on their way.

Amsterdam. Hmm. Paul had heard some 'stories' and therefore knew a little about it, or thought he did. Denis, well he knew all about the windmills and the clogs and cheese and he'd vaguely heard of Ann Frank, who wasn't to feature on 'Blue Peter' for another three years. Des, being more of a science student had just about heard of it.

"Wow! This is different." said Des as they first caught sight of Amsterdam's major feature, its historic canals.

"Yes apparently there are 165 of them running through it." said Denis helpfully.

"And blimey, everybody is riding a bicycle!" continued Des.

It was getting to commuter time as the bus pulled into Amsterdam and yes, it seemed everybody was riding a bicycle.

"That's mad." said Paul, with his nose pressed against the glass.

Once again with Marten's assistance, who had phoned through to ensure that they had spaces for the night, the boys soon found the hostel (what had happened to camping under the stars and cooking on an open log fire lads?), which this time, was very close to the city centre, and after a quick wash and brush up, they were ready to hit the town.

"I must say, I am liking these hostels." said Denis whose own experience in England had been a rather strict affair with rows of bunks.

"And you had to do a job in the morning before you could leave!" he added.

In this rather upmarket affair, the boys had their own room, though as they discovered when they were leaving, this was reflected in the cost. The rapidly dwindling funds were fast emerging as a source of concern. The camping au naturel and the al fresco dining had given way to hot showers and decent meals. Though in Denis's defence, his own that is, he had buckled under the pressure of his companions and the lure of a warm bed.

Anyway, that could all wait until tomorrow.

"I could really do with a beer." declared Paul, and the others couldn't argue with that.

So tumbling out of the oddly named, ClinkNOORD Hostel, they found themselves just about in the middle of Amsterdam. After wasting no time admiring the amazingly tall buildings with their magnificent colours which lined the various canals, and other fascinating features of this old town, they went into a bar.

Now the boys although being well-seasoned heavy drinkers of at least two pints of a lager on a Friday night, had little knowledge of Dutch beer, but Denis informed them that it was originally brewed by monks, or was that Belgium beer, which wasn't really helpful, but they all agreed that the Grolsch sounded local, which it was, and also 5%. Oh dear.

Three pints, because they were on holiday, later. They kind of stumbled out of the establishment armed with the helpful advice of a bunch of young Amsterdamians (probably not a word) with whom, as the evening had progressed, and the beers…

"Large?"

"Oh yes please."

…had been sunk, they had struck up a friendship.

"How come everybody speaks English so well?" said Des.

"Goodness knows, I guess everyone wants to." suggested Paul.

"Down here they said.", remembered Denis pointing, as they went straight into the 'Red Light District.'

"Wow! WOW!! Look at that!"

Draped in what appeared to be an innocent-looking shop window, was a young lady leaving little to the imagination as to what lay behind her flimsy negligée.

"Bloody 'ell" gasped Denis, eyes popping out.

Spotting perhaps a potential client, the young lady pouted provocatively towards Des whose jaw immediately dropped in unison with Denis's.

"That's it, that's it, that's what my cousin told me!" Paul shouted jumping up and down gleefully.

"He told me that!"

The young lady on witnessing the antics of Paul immediately recognised the potential clients for what they were and spoke to someone behind her. In the meantime, while Des and Denis stood frozen, Paul had progressed further down the line of 'shops' and standing outside another one, shouted,

"Whoa look at this one!! Cor!!"

At that moment two doors opened. One to the right of Paul and one to the left of Denis and Des. Out of which flew two very large, 'managers' who recognising three drunken foreign voyeurs staring at their merchandise with no intention to purchase, proceeded, at speed to rearrange their stupid faces.

Fortunately, their huge frames, designed more for close encounters, were no match for the speed of the boys who were fuelled up on a mixture of Grolsch and adrenalin. Even so, it was still some time before they managed to shake off their raging pursuers. Unfortunately, whilst Denis and Des scarpered one way, Paul had to escape in the other direction.

After an hour or so and with no sign of Paul, the boys made their way back to the hostel, where of course they found Paul. Due to a mixture of beer, fear and the physics of a large quantity of gassy liquid being bounced up and down the streets of Amsterdam, Denis immediately threw up in the sink.

By the time the police arrived at the scene of the drama and taken a few details, this carefully controlled feature of this very organised city had returned to its usual calm. The young ladies once again sat smiling sweetly at their more usual, discreet, potential clients.

Back at the hostel, Denis struggling to find the right page in his, 'I Spy' book, finally drifted off to sleep,

The next day didn't start too well either, despite the 'upmarket' nature of the hostel, the bed didn't include breakfast. Paul discovered this first when he went to ask the not-so-helpful man on the desk, where breakfast was.

"In town." came the dismissive response.

"In town?" Paul asked before twigging.

"Well we got it in the last one." responded Paul failing to hide his indignation. "And, and it was cheaper than this place."

"Does it say breakfast included? Read your, 'Welcome Pack'." responded the not-so-helpful man on the desk, totally missing the irony.

It didn't take too long however before they managed to find a promising place for breakfast and not too far away.

"Look there's a place." said Denis. "Happy Hippy Coffee Shop. I've heard of those coffee shops, apparently they're quite a feature of Amsterdam."

They opened the door of the rather smoky café, and, courtesy of the friendly young boy at the counter, delighted at the opportunity to practice his English, were soon sitting down with three steaming bowls of milky coffee and three large slices of thick bread, covered in peanut butter.

Tucking into their peanut butter doorsteps, the boys a little more relaxed now, it may have well been the smoke, began to mull over the previous evening's close encounter with death.

"Cor, they like a smoke with their breakfasts here don't they." observed Des, noticing the big fat cigarettes being enjoyed by most of the other customers.

At that point just like his Biblical namesake, well not quite the same, Paul had a sudden revelation but it was too late.

Alerted by a raised voice at the counter, the boys looked up to see a rather agitated-looking coffee shop owner berating his young son.

"Five minutes I left you, you know the rules!"

"Smoking?" he said turning his attention to the group of young foreigners sitting around the table

"Sthorry?" Denis tried to respond with his mouth cloying up with peanut butter.

"Oh, er no thanks, we don't actually, thanks anyway." he continued rather bemused.

"Smart Alec eh? So why are you here?" demanded the patron.

"Passports!"

"Erm, they're back at the hostel. Why?"

"You need ID, you have to be over eighteen to be here." the owner's voice was becoming agitated.

"We are." assured Des.

"I'm actually nineteen." added Paul, thinking that might help.

"Why would we need ID in a café." thought Denis, "we weren't even asked at the bar last night."

"Out! Out!" the raised voice of the owner signalling that time for discussion was officially over.

Quickly swigging the last of the coffee and grabbing handfuls of sticky bread, the boys immediately stood up and scrambled for the door.

That's when the Police came in.

"Oh great!" groaned Mr Patron seeing his licence disappearing, literally in a puff of smoke.

"Great!"

Dressed immaculately in their dark uniforms and each carrying a pistol, the two officers wasted no time in carrying out their duties, starting with the three young foreigners attempting to leave.

"Three young foreigners." the younger officer thought to himself. "Hmm."

The owner immediately began a stream of conversation which ebbed and flowed between him and the two officers, one of whom was strategically placed by the door. Every so often he would point at his young son then at the boys and then back to his son, who was by this time, visibly shrinking. Finally terminating the animated conversation with the delivery of a clear rebuke to the owner, whose expression a mixture of contrition and relief suggested that his livelihood had survived, the Policeman turned his attentions to the boys.

"Passports." he demanded, very professional and business-like.

"Hm ah yes," stuttered Denis, the spokesman, "er we didn't know and they are all back at the hostel where we are staying."

"We are from England." he added, expecting that this little nugget of information may help.

"Er English."

"ID's." demanded the officer, obviously unimpressed.

"Erm, yes." responded Denis now squirming. "Yes er we don't have those in England, well er actually we do have International Youth Hostel ID cards but er hm they are back there too. Er, at the hostel"

"You know that in Holland it is a criminal offence not to carry ID?" the officer began in perfect English.

"Do you know that in Amsterdam it is illegal for anyone under 18 to enter an establishment of this nature?"

Des was about to say, but we are 18, then thought better of it.

Turning sharply, the officer made one final acerbic comment to the shop owner and then leaving his colleague to complete the checks, he proceeded to escort the chastened companions back to the hostel.

'Mr Grumpy', was not best pleased to see his foreign guests arriving back accompanied by a Police Officer and immediately made his displeasure clear.

After satisfying himself that the miscreants were indeed over

18, the policeman delivered a final witheringly clear warning, concluding by reminding them how fortunate both they and the coffee shop owner were, to find him in such a compassionate mood. And marched out.

"I want you out." said the man behind the desk.

"Your behaviour is not good," he continued stymieing any protests from the boys.

"Last night you came back late and noisy, one of you I heard you being sick in the room and now you bring back the Police. This is a respectable establishment. You are lucky I don't charge you for tonight. Get your bags. Goodbye!"

Sometime later, sitting in the station waiting room and pondering their next move, Des broke the silence.

 "You seem to have known a lot about Amsterdam." he said, reflecting on Paul's earlier revelation about the sudden moment of enlightenment he had experienced in the café.

 "Yeh, shame you never shared them with us." added Denis.

Time for the map boys?

Despite the fact that most of the cash they had left was Deutsch Marks, for some reason they didn't fancy Germany, nothing really sprung to mind there. So they sat staring at a bit of a loss. They dismissed going further north to the Scandinavian countries as they had already decided that it was getting rather cold and having set out believing that abroad was always warm, they had not really packed any warm clothing.

 "Well Alan Whicker, any ideas for our next European delight?" Denis sarcastically asked Paul, their Amsterdam tour guide,

"Well." he said. "Look what I have spotted, Luxembourg! And we all know what's there."

"Radio Lux-em-bourg!!" they all sang in unison. And proceeded to catch the last train to Luxembourg, literally.

And that's how they ended up in Metz. Yes Metz, somewhere in Northern France.

Well, they caught the train to Luxembourg all right but it didn't pull into the station until after midnight, however, this time they did successfully spend the night stretched out in the station waiting room.

The next morning they found a hostel, which seemed to be built into the rock, down in the bowels of the old town.

After exploring the city of Luxembourg, which confusingly had the same name as the country, and finding no trace of Radio Luxembourg, they concluded that the city had even less to offer than Belgium and having done a quick audit of their resources decided that the siren call of Bordeaux with surely warmer weather and a chance to earn some money, could no longer be resisted.

The next morning in relatively high spirits, though slightly dampened by the atrocious weather, they made their way to the nearest auto-route to hitch a lift to Bordeaux some 625 miles south. Two hours and a mere 55 miles later, they were dropped off on the end of a slip road of the main route south, close to the town of Metz. As it was pouring with rain they decided to break the journey hoping conditions might improve, it was still relatively early. They managed to locate a café which looked like a large old house in the middle of nowhere, surrounded by swirling mist and rain and motorways.

Denis was buoyed up a little when in perfect French he ordered,

"Trois café au laits. "S'il vous plait, madame."

"Now that's progress." he thought.

Madame was touched and smiled at the bedraggled group of friends huddled around the table.

"That's it, I'm not hitching anymore. I've had it." declared Paul, "I'm not. Look at the way that lorry driver looked at us as we struggled to get us and all our gear into his cab. Who's gonna give us a lift? I think that's why he said he wasn't going any further and dropped us off in the middle of nowhere. 'Ave bloody had it!"

Denis and Des could hardly disagree, but they seemed more conscious of their dwindling funds. Paul did seem to have brought rather more than them and they suspected that he may have been subsidised by his parents. He had been the first to abandon the idea of camping, something the other two found hard to resist after their first night's experience but it had hit their budget very hard.

It looked like Paul might be about to abandon ship.

"OK." said Denis. "Look why don't we see if we can get a student ticket south, straight to Bordeaux? If we can just get jobs grape picking. Those Canadians said that they give you food and shelter as well as pay you. What do you think?"

They all agreed that it would be a shame if the adventure were to end so soon and Paul said that he was willing to give it a go,

"But I'm not hitching again!" he added.

"Ask the lady behind the counter Denis," suggested Des, "she seems nice."

"Oh this'll be fun thought Denis."

But the nice lady who had served them the coffee had overheard some of their conversation and understood the gist of it. As he approached the counter she said,

"Zer is a train from Paris. My 'usband can drop you at Gare de Metz. He is going zer soon. You can take a train to Paris and then overnight to Bordeaux. Will I ask 'im?"

And she did.

"Attention les Nomads!!" Le 'usband shouted after the boys, as he left them on the concourse of the station.

"What was that?" asked Paul.

"Dunno." answered Denis

After the purchase of the tickets for the journey had relieved Des and Denis of most of their remaining funds, they realised that it was imperative that they managed to quickly find the grape picking work.

It would have helped had they had time to check their ticket to see which was the correct door to board the train, but an overzealous guard had hurriedly bundled them on. So, climbing on board, the three travellers struggled down the endless narrow corridor of the train, in search of their allocated couchette, with Des and particularly Denis, banging their bulky haversacks against most of the doors as they went. However, after a while, hearing the howls of indignation which poured out of the various couchettes, what had started off as a source of some embarrassment soon became a source of intense amusement. It appeared that some passengers were already in bed!!

When they finally found their compartment, it was a little underwhelming. OK, they hadn't expected a large roomy suite, but with the added encumbrance of their bags, to say that space was tight was a generous description.

Immediately in response to seeing two sets of narrow bunks. Paul announced,

"I can't sleep on top. I get dizziness"

Whilst Des had already plonked his haversack on the other bottom bed.

"Fine." said Denis, with a sense of the inevitable,

"Cor there's not much room is there?" said Des, kind of stating the obvious.

"All we need now.." but before he could continue with. "is for someone else to come in for that bed."

The door slid back and in walked a rather large French fellow, who immediately began directing at the boys a stream of something unintelligible, at which Des and Paul looked at Denis, who immediately defaulted to his usual response and answered,

"Oui."

To which the rather large gentleman, said something which sounded like 'good', and, much to his dismay, plonked his bag down on Paul's bed.

Denis managed to conceal a smile, but only just.

After managing to clamber into their respective bunks and finally settle down, the rather large gentleman began to produce some rather large snoring, which continued unabated for most of the night. It also soon became clear that the size of the compartment was not only physically challenging but neither did it contain enough oxygen for the requirements of four people. Apart from Paul, whose 'dizziness' seemed to be having a positive side-effect, the other two lay for most of the night in a state of semi-consciousness.

The next morning as they were approaching Bordeaux, and even though it was shortly after dawn, it was with some relief that a steward came in to return the couchettes back to seats. This was quickly followed by a ticket inspector, who on checking the ticket of the rather large gentleman, who turned out not to be French after all, started his own stream of rather animated conversation which resulted in the gentleman being summarily despatched back to the carriage he was supposed to have been in in the first place.

As they headed in the direction of the hostel, which they had managed to locate via the station tourist office, they were looking forward to a shower and a good sleep before going in search of grape picking the next day. When they had enquired about it at the tourist office the young lady at the desk had just laughed and waved her arms saying.

"Everywhere!"

But as they hesitated to check on the little map with the hostel marked on it, they were approached by a shady-looking man in a grubby suit who said,

"Vous voudriez vendange?"

"Er English." responded Des before Denis could reply.

"You want grape pick?"

The boys looked at each other torn between exhaustion and a stroke of good fortune. But before they could arrive at a consensus, he had made their decision for them.

"Come." he said, and they followed him around the corner to a large vehicle which looked a bit like a furniture van. Ushered into the back, the door was immediately rolled down behind them and after a few minutes of complete darkness, the light from a skylight in the roof began to reveal the inside. A jumble of old blankets, a car tyre, various tools and most disturbingly, a shotgun fastened to the far wall, and looking around further the boys could see that the walls of the van were stained red! Had they not at the same time noticed the pannier baskets also scattered around, they would have completely freaked out.

The van screeched away and after a journey of over an hour, which, whilst being tossed around in the back, seemed to go on forever, the boys wondered if it would ever end. Just as they were about to implement plan 'B', which they didn't actually have, they came to an abrupt halt.

The door rolled up and dazzled by the sudden brightness they more or less fell out. As their sight returned, they realised that they were in some sort of encampment with lots of people milling around staring at them curiously. Kids were playing, there was a smoky fire next to a large stone building and there were a variety of old vehicles including a tractor and a pile of old tyres, it all looked a bit haphazard. The untidy-looking man who had first approached them was talking to a very large man, obviously the boss, with a face which he appeared, on several occasions, to have hit a baseball bat with.

The conversation, which to the boys was completely unintelligible, did include the word English, which elicited a cursory grunt from the big guy. It didn't bode well. Their previous experiences of being frozen in France, stared at in Paris, and positively abused in Amsterdam, suddenly felt quite homely.

Clearly expecting them to follow, he led them over to the large stone building and opened the door onto a single room with a straw-covered floor. The room was lined all around the edges by what seemed to be, 'gentlemen of the road', some lounging, some sleeping and some just staring.

"I think this is where we are meant to sleep." said Denis. "Thank God we've got the tent."

He then took them over to a little construction which housed a 'long-drop' toilet, (provide your own paper!) and next to that, a tap.

And finally to a long table containing tonight's supper. Plates of little fish complete with heads and tails, piles of bread and a container full of some sort of soup.

Bon appetit!

Denis had a sudden and disturbing recollection of the last thing that one of the Canadians, after painting such a positive picture, had said to him about grape picking,

"But once you've started with a team, you do have to stay until the end."

Having pitched the tent a little way from the general mêlée, they had quickly retreated inside to sleep. Supper came and went but they continued to sleep until morning, food was the last thing on their minds.

At seven in the morning they were awakened by shouts of, "Allez! Allez!" and on leaving the tent, joined the other pickers at the table which contained breakfast. Despite the situation, having foregone food the previous day they were actually starving, and despite the continued presence of the little fish, the milky coffee and bread and jam were quite recognisable as breakfast, so they made the most of it. Which was just as well.

Work started at 8 am sharp and continued non-stop until 12 noon when they paused for a lunch break of two hours, before continuing all the way through until 6pm.

The menacing mood of the previous evening created by the surly guy with the broken face continued throughout the day.

Positioning himself at the end of the grape vines, and with several equally threatening helpers, the emphasis was very clearly on speed. No slacking was tolerated. Each picker was supplied with a pair of secateurs and a basket and expected to make their way from one end of a row of grapes to the other, filling the basket as they went. When the basket was full, they would tip the contents into a large pannier carried on leather straps by another worker who in turn, when that was full, tipped it into a wagon, to be taken to the wine press.

The process was very organised and carefully monitored. There was very little conversation, everybody was busily concentrating on avoiding the displeasure of the big man, who at one point began to seriously berate a very old man who was obviously struggling to keep up to speed.

"Bloody hell! Did you see that?" whispered Paul. "He was

swinging that big club around that bloke's head."

Des and Denis, looking at each other aghast, certainly had.

By midday the boys were exhausted, their backs aching from continuous bending and their limbs sore from lifting the baskets up to empty into the panniers. At one point Paul, who decided that it might be easier to not fill the basket too full, was subjected to a torrent of angry abuse by one of the youths watching the pickers. After that, he made well sure that his basket was full.

Lunch was fish and soup, as was supper.

Ominously, the old man who had been the subject of the boss's ire did not appear for the afternoon session and the exhausting routine continued monotonously until 6pm when the three companions collapsed onto the grass outside their tent.

They would have probably remained there all night except that the various children, who up to now had simply viewed the English boys with curiosity, had begun to become a little more intrusive. Casually picking up the boys' bags and any possessions lying around and becoming less jocular in their various comments, which invariably contained the word, Eeenglish. The boys decided to once again retreat to the relative safety of their tent.

It was time to make a plan.

"I can't take any more of this." said Paul, clearly speaking for all three of them.

"You're not kidding!" agreed Des, "They're bloody nutters."

"Well we definitely can't go and tell them that we are leaving."

said Denis.

But the other two had already gathered that.

Thank goodness they had chosen to pitch a distance away from the main hub. The plan was simple. They would pack up everything immediately. As soon as it was dark they would pull all the pegs out of the tent and sit tight until after midnight when they would quietly roll the tent up and carry it out through the main entrance. Des didn't like the idea of the main entrance, to which they agreed, so they decided to cut through the grape vines and hopefully find a passage onto the main road a bit further down.

At half-past midnight, everything was absolute silence and they were literally ready to roll when they heard a noise outside of the tent. A shuffling at first, caused them all to hold their breath. And then horrendous coughing, then silence and then the unmistakable sound of someone with diarrhoea evacuating their bowels and then after more shuffling, again complete silence.

Resisting the urge to react, they prudently, though with difficulty, waited for about twenty minutes until they were sure everything was once again still.

"Let's go." whispered Denis.

Fortunately, there was a bit of a moon and they were able to see enough to roll up the tent without any difficulty and head straight for the lines of grape vines. Feeling relatively safe there, they lay for a few moments listening to the silence before continuing.

Surging with adrenalin, they headed to where they believed the main road was and thank God it was. By now being obstructed by a large hedge was not a serious obstacle and they simply ploughed through it and onto the road. Fortunately, Paul was able to remind them that on the last part of the journey they had all slipped to the back of the van as it went up a steep hill, they set off down the hill with a feeling of elation.

As they made progress they were beginning to believe that it was over and just a matter of time before they reached some kind of village. But then the lights of a vehicle appeared heading their way. The bend in the road made it difficult to gauge in which direction the lights were coming from, but at one o'clock in the morning, it was likely to be either to or from the camp. Elation quickly turned to panic. Were they coming looking for them, or returning from a night out? Either way, it wasn't good and they dived straight into the ditch at the side of the road and hoped and prayed that they were completely concealed. The vehicle sped past and disappeared into the distance, but all the same, the boys lay in the ditch for some time before continuing.

As dawn began to break they had been walking for several hours and with the effects of the adrenalin beginning to wear off, were well and truly knackered. Thankfully, they could see in the distance the welcome sight of a church spire which indicated that a village was not far away and being so close to habitation, their fears of being apprehended began to subside. However as they were considering that there was still some distance to go, a vehicle pulled up beside them. Thankfully not a van but a little Citroen 2 CV, driven by a little old lady, and however unlikely it seemed, though they didn't understand a word she was saying, she was obviously offering them a lift.

Gratefully they piled into the tiny car, bags and all, whilst repeating,

"Oh merci, madame, merci!"

Dropping them off in the village, they sat on a kerb stone at the side of the road planning their next move. At which point a little old lady, a different one, came up to them and dropped a ten franc piece into each of their hands before wandering off. The boys just stared at each other, shocked. Des promptly burst into tears, though he forever after denied it. The emotion of the episode of the previous 48 hours having been contrasted with two spontaneous examples of the milk of human kindness, was too much, and crying or not, it was a while before any of them spoke.

From then on, like some religious shrine, it was always referred to affectionately as the 'Village of the Two Old Ladies.'

They were still desperate to replenish their funds but also needed to sort out accommodation for the night. A return to the hostel in Bordeaux seemed to be the only solution, at least for now. An immediate visit to the village boulangerie provided them, not only with sustenance, but having just enough English, the boulanger was also able to provide information about a bus to Bordeaux which they were soon spread out on the back seat of, fast asleep. It brought from most of the freshly alighting passengers, several shrugs of French indignation, to which the three companions were happily oblivious.

So after a journey of two hours or so, and approximately just 48 hours since their initial visit they were sitting in the common room of the hostel in Bordeaux, in front of three cups of milky coffee and one pastry between them. That's when Monsieur Goulven appeared.

Dressed in a bottle green corduroy jacket and brown slacks, Monsieur Goulven resembled a very smart country gentleman. As he approached the boys, his black curls and tanned skin, gave the appearance of someone suave and sophisticated.

"Do you want to pick grapes?" he said without introduction.

The response from the boys was understandably delayed as each one, startled by the question, tried to formulate a suitable answer. The awkward silence was eventually broken by Denis who proceeded to provide Monsieur Goulven with an animated and detailed account of the previous 48 hours of their lives.

At the end of which Monsieur Goulven smiled and said,

"Ah, les Nomads"

"Nomads!" repeated Denis. "Nomads! That's what that bloke in Metz shouted after us, watch out for Nomads!"

Monsieur Goulven proceeded to tell them that they had been picked up by an organised group, who take on the vendange, or grape picking, on behalf of the proprietor of a Château and are paid by him to organise the recruitment of workers and completion of the harvest. It is quite common, though rather lazy and can also, in many ways, be less than satisfactory. You were very lucky, the last thing they would allow you to do is leave early before the harvest is complete.

In response to Monsieur Goulven's last remark, the boys felt a little sick.

"Things at Château Bel Vue will be very different." he continued. "I will provide you with good food and accommodation, and I will pay you properly. It will probably take about six weeks to complete and I hope, but not force, that you will stay until the end."

It was in many ways a difficult decision. But then again Monsieur Goulven was no shady guy in a scruffy suit and certainly not a big fat guy with a broken face and a club. He spoke very good

English and seemed to be genuinely charming. The Canadian guys had spoken with great enthusiasm about grape picking so maybe they had just been unlucky, or lucky! Plus they had just about spent their last money on the night's accommodation in the hostel. It seemed that they didn't really have a lot of choices.

"Look." he said, understanding their qualms. "Have a good night's sleep here in the hostel. Tomorrow is Friday. I will come along in the afternoon, then if you want to, I will take you to the Château."

After this final piece of reassurance, the boys were pretty much decided and the next day they climbed into Monsieur Goulven's large land-rover and set off on their next adventure.

"Oh boy!"

As they drove up the drive of Monsieur Goulven's residence, the Château Bel-Vue stood resplendent before them. Beyond it to the sides and behind it, rows and rows of grape vines stretched for as far as the eye could see, sweeping down to the tree line in the distance. In the front of the main house were beautifully manicured gardens, which despite being well into autumn, still retained some colour. The whole picture suggested order and organisation. If the boys had harboured any doubts about their decision to accept Monsieur Goulven's invitation, it had by now disappeared.

Taking them inside, Monsieur Goulven introduced them to his wife Eva, an impossibly good-looking woman with the face of a painted doll, and their two children Amelie and Henri who were dressed like they had just walked off the cat-walk of a children's fashion show. After swapping pleasantries, during which the boys struggled not to continually stare at Eva, they were shown upstairs to their room, a huge place with three beds. After showing them the bathroom, Monsieur Goulven told them to make themselves at home, have a shower and a rest, and then come for supper at 1800 hours.

"6 o'clock." whispered Denis.

"The Château is located close to the town of Belves-de-Castillon in the valley of the Dordogne river. We are in the department of the Gironde and around 60 miles from Bordeaux." Monsieur Goulven was telling them at supper.

"As you can see." he continued with a smile, "We are fairly isolated here, so if you did want to escape, the closest town for transport links is Libourne, about 20 kilometres to the west."

Sensing that their experience with, 'les Nomads', was probably still raw, he said something in French to Eva, who though she couldn't speak English, immediately began to reassure their guests whilst playfully scolding her husband.

The meal was to the boys something of an experience, with cheeses and pâtées never before encountered, and a curious starter, which the boys did not even recognise. In front of each of them were a globe artichoke and a dish of what appeared to be oil. Monsieur Goulven explained that they should pull a thick leaf off the artichoke and after dipping into the olive oil should, scrape off the flesh with their teeth. The main course of pork in a cream sauce, although recognisable, was certainly not familiar, but delicious, and then curiously before the dessert of Caneles de Bordeaux with ice cream, they were invited to sample a variety of cheeses.

It was clear that the boys were something of a curiosity to the Goulven family and they were very much enjoying both entertaining and being entertained by them. Monsieur Goulven encouraged Amelie and Henri to try out their few words of English and as the meal progressed and the various wines took hold, Denis wasn't allowing his limited command of French to restrict his willingness to use it. His companions, rather than being in any way put out by his apparent display of competence, were actually really impressed and kept asking him what he'd just said.

"Oh you know, this and that." he replied casually.

They didn't really notice that what Denis said in French was exclusively directed at Monsieur Goulven, and not at his wife and children. Happily, Monsieur Goulven's own command of English ensured continuity, and he very kindly did not give any indication that much of Denis's conversation didn't actually make a lot of sense.

Eventually, by the time the evening reached its conclusion, it had been a great success for both parties.

Later that night, Denis lay in his wonderfully comfortable bed considering how their fortunes had changed in just a short time. Falling asleep, he dreamt of sitting proudly in his chair in the centre of a room, chewing on artichokes and handing out pearls of wisdom in French, to an audience hungry for his wisdom, and sitting at his feet were Des and Paul.

They had realised that the accommodation in the main house had only been temporary, but it was still with some reluctance, that on the Sunday they transferred to a converted barn, kitted out for the workers with rows of single beds. Though not exactly the Châteaux, it was however, very clean and comfortable and being the first ones there, they were also able to choose the premium places near the windows.

"Allez les braves!" was a phrase that they were to become very familiar with over the next few weeks when at 7am the following morning, Monsieur Goulven called the morning reveille for their first day's grape picking.

After their previous toils in the grape vines, the boys were really not looking forward to the day's grape picking, but as it turned out several factors resulted in a great improvement in the experience.
For a start, the vines were at a different height which meant that they could be accessed without bending down to cut the stems.

Beginning at the bottom of the row on their knees they were able to shuffle steadily along without having to stand until they reached the top of the row. Though it was a bit rough on the knees, the ground being not too hard, made it tolerable and it was certainly an improvement on the back-breaking nature of their first experience. This slightly slowed the process down, but then this was another improvement in that neither was the manic sense of urgency apparent. The other big bonus was that plenty of chatter went on between the various pickers as they worked, which also helped to lighten the burden enormously. With the constant banter and the assistance provided by routine, the time seemed to fly by and after a short break halfway through the morning, it was soon midday and their first morning's work completed.

They were exhausted but happily so.

After a two-hour break they were ready to go again and after overcoming an uncomfortable start, were soon back in the comfort zone of routine.

They had been joined at the start of the morning by several other pickers, mainly local French people, and also four people who would later join them in the accommodation block and stayed with them throughout the harvest. These were Jean-Pierre, a formidable French guy with a huge beard. A couple of French hippy types in their twenties, Celeste and Bowie, who were really gentle people, and also a French-speaking native of French Guyana, called Azori, who provided much entertainment with his vivacious personality, which did at times irritate the far more sober Jean-Pierre, causing some awkward moments, but he never irritated the boys who loved him. Over the coming weeks, they would all become very good friends and it was from these encounters that the boys', particularly Denis's, French, improved enormously, though some words he wouldn't have learnt at school anyway.

That evening they were also joined by a girl from Australia who was 'doing' Europe. Her name was Lucy, a strapping blonde from Brisbane and at twenty-five, which was even older than Denis's sister, became a bit of a mother figure to the boys. Denis and Lucy became particularly close friends over the weeks as they both shared a rather romantic view of the world, though the 'romance' bit remained strictly their view of the world, she was twenty-five for goodness sake!!

The week usually ended at noon on Saturday though they also had Wednesday afternoon off, an arrangement, the boys used to their weekends, struggled to see the logic in,

"Must just be a French thing." Denis said.

All of the pickers were fed by the hosts at lunchtimes and the resident pickers were also provided with a substantial evening meal. On Wednesday and Saturday evenings and Sundays however, they were expected to provide meals for themselves, using the facilities in the common room to cook on.

Wednesday lunchtime therefore, and also on a Saturday morning, the boys were able to place an order with Madame Goulven, who on these days went into Belves-de Castillon, for anything that they wished to purchase from the shops, the cost of which was deducted from their wages.

Unfortunately, the boys, who were used to their tea usually appearing magically on the table, and with their recently acquired culinary knowledge being restricted to just about, bread, cheese and sometimes ham, apart from these items they didn't really know what to buy, so it was therefore mainly confection.

As time went by they were assisted in food preparation by the others, mainly Azori, who also introduced them to cayenne pepper, which he would scatter liberally on his tongue. The boys, however, only experienced it once, though the effects of it lasted for hours.

Strangely because the rest of the week was so busy, Sunday could drag a bit, but they were provided with some entertainment by the cassette recorder and tapes Denis had brought, and their French cousins loved to listen to the English pop music. Even though the batteries had long since run out they managed to make the recorder work by sticking the two wires into the shaving plug above the sink, which was all a little haphazard, and resulted in regular electric shocks!

Azori was a keen learner of English, though he did rather overuse the phrase,

"I am gladee."

The boys helpfully did introduce him to other English words and expressions including,

".. probably the worst English swear word that you could imagine…bubbly gum." before recoiling in horror whenever he repeated it.

Naughty boys!

As time went by, new people came and went, including a very weird chap called Claud, who wearing thick black-rimmed glasses and dressed improbably in a suit more fitting for a meeting of shabby businessmen than for grape picking, spent the two nights he stayed pouring over some extremely dodgy magazines before disappearing as suddenly as he had arrived, with, it has to be said, some relief to the boys. A very pleasant addition to the group was a young Irish girl called Orlaith who was wandering around France in search of material for her poetry. She had a fascination for sloths, with, as it became apparent, good reason, and found the intensity of grape picking far too prosaic. After a week she too drifted away in much the same way as she had arrived. Denis the romantic was sad to see her go, Des and Paul thought she was freaky.

On several occasions on their afternoons off, Monsieur Goulven, invited the boys to get involved around the grounds of the Château. There was no obligation but they were very happy to, as it did help to pass the 'down-time', mind you picking grapes was exhausting work and getting up at 7am every day wasn't something that came naturally to them, so they spent a lot of their free time asleep.

Monsieur Goulven had explained to the boys that his relatively small enterprise was part of a local Cooperative whereby the grapes from his vendange went to a central point to be turned into bottles of France's most famous export. There was security in this arrangement as it meant that the local Patrons were able to support each other better, sharing resources like the expensive machinery of processing and of course labour. It also created a much less pressured environment which led to a happier workforce, which in turn meant that the pickers tended to stay loyal until the end of the harvest.

"It did however mean," he informed them with some regret

"that the label on his bottles of wine stated, 'Mis en bouteille au domain' and not at the Château and therefore the wine in his bottles of 'Château Bel Vue', was sadly not actually exclusive to the Château Bel Vue."

Although," he added forcefully,

"It certainly does not compromise the quality."

On one Wednesday afternoon, he took them to the main processing hub of the Cooperative, to see what happened to the grapes once the large open trailer had transported them. It turned out to be a fascinating experience, though Denis was surprised to discover that no water was added to the wine during the process, it was pure grape juice. He was about to ask Monsieur Goulven about this, but impressed by the Patron's obvious passion for both the process and its end product, decided to remain prudently silent. Probably just as well Denis mate!!

Denis did get to enjoy something that he had been desperate to do ever since the Canadian boys had suggested grape picking, trampling grapes with his bare feet. He'd seen it on an old Pathe Newsreel about France and Wine Production in one of the few school geography lessons he had enjoyed. Monsieur Goulven laughed when he asked about it. The process of grape crushing was now carried out in a large container that resembled an upside-down flat-bottomed pyramid containing a huge screw which forced the grapes onto a large plate at the end, squeezing out every last drop of juice. However, there were several grand oak-panelled, 'holding barrels', full of grapes waiting to be crushed and Monsieur invited Denis to climb in and crush away. Denis was thrilled at the opportunity and quickly relieving himself of his socks and shoes climbed right in. His less romantically inclined companions however, didn't quite see the attraction in it and declined the invitation to join him.

The routine of the days' early rises and the monotony of the picking, meant that the weeks flew by, and towards the end of the harvest they were joined by a large number of Spanish pickers who were following the grape harvest over the Pyrènees mountains. They added a new welcome texture to the group of workers and also considerably speeded things up. Before long with a mixture of great excitement and relief, but also some regret, the vendange was complete.

They had spent the last six weeks in close proximity to their new companions and they had all grown very close. They knew that departure would bring some sadness, but before that and in celebration of the conclusion of the harvest, Monsieur Goulven organised a huge paella feast, another first for the boys. It all looked very impressive, except for the mussels which the boys had never even seen before, and certainly had no intention of trying, well at least not until Azori had convinced Denis, of course, that they provided a culinary experience far greater than their appearance suggested. Denis, to be honest, was not totally sold, however it was another milestone for him, and in later years he would enjoy many a 'moules frites'.

From day one of the vendanges, the pickers, were able to access a daily allowance of a bottle of wine each, which, being more used to weak lager was to the boys never really an attraction. However they did have an odd tipple, and this, though never becoming a bottle a day, did increase in volume as time went by. By the time they were enjoying the paella feast and with the encouragement of the company and mood of the evening, they managed to indulge in more than that particular day's allowance. That is how the next morning Denis awoke to find himself lying between two grape vines some distance from the Château, and not having a clue how he had arrived there.

It was quite a sombre morning when they all finally went their separate ways. The boys thanked Monsieur and Madame Goulven for their kindness and in turn hugged their new friends. Denis said a special goodbye to Lucy and they promised to keep in touch, which they did for a while, but Denis and his companions never saw any of them again.

Very kindly Monsieur Goulven drove the boys to the railway station in Bordeaux. Now that they were in possession of a pocket full of cash they didn't even consider hitchhiking, for now anyway, and were heading by train for Genoa in Italy to continue their journey to teach English in Turkey, something Lucy had suggested, and then that kibbutz thing.

It was however no surprise to Denis and Des when as they entered the station Paul announced that he had had enough adventures and was heading back to England.

Denis and Des, a little down-beat, climbed on board the train and headed East, but that's another story.

Denis did return to visit the Château many years later with Maisie, and his children, Clare and Jack, but by then the Château was no longer lived in, the grape vines had been bought out by a large English supermarket. The Goulvens had only the previous year retired closer to Bordeaux, and the harvest was now done largely by machine.

It was a very emotional day for Denis, and sensing this, Maisie left him to his thoughts, accompanied, of course, by a bottle of local red wine.

◆ ◆ ◆

Denis was slowly returning back to the land of the living. But he wasn't finished yet……….....

CHAPTER 5

It was one of those serendipity moments that had kicked it all off, more explicitly his neighbour mowing his front lawn. Denis was sitting at home, the sun shining in through the window which, being slightly ajar, allowed the aroma of newly cut grass to drift in. The normal Denis response would have been.

"Oh for goodness sake! Why are you cutting your grass in March?"

But before that particular rail could emerge it was quickly derailed by the distinctive scent which immediately evoked romantic thoughts of the outdoors and camping.

"It's a camper we need." thought Denis, "as his romantic thoughts developed. "Maisie ain't gonna go for a tent anymore and anyway the old trailer tent had long since fallen apart. Yeh, one of those trailers that turn into half a caravan, cooker, sink, even a fridge."

"You mean a caravan." suggested the very practical Maisie, when he later shared his idea with her.

"No, not a caravan, you may as well go away in a house on bloody wheels."

"Yes that's it Denis, now you are talking."

Maisie was only being half-serious. She always liked to challenge her husband's more romantic notions before giving them her assent. One, simply because she could, and more importantly because she knew that she would be very much involved in the practical side of enabling them to actually work.

It hadn't taken very long to locate a very good 'folding camper', in excellent condition, and at a reasonable price, being sold by a slightly older couple who felt that it was getting a bit much for them but that they had had lots of fun in it and had kept it immaculate, which they had, kept it immaculate.

After going on a couple of trial runs locally, to 'get used' to their new acquisition, i.e. how to put it up, Denis and Maisie were poised to head off on a trip that Denis had long since contemplated. To set out in September, at the end of the holiday season, and take their time, to meander their way down through France to Jack's in the South. Weeks? Months? Who knows? Who even cares?

They had in fact attempted the trip two years earlier, but due to unseasonal gales and endless sideways rain, the meandering weeks or months ended up as barely four soggy nights. It was finally terminated when they awoke one morning to discover that their previous evening's deserted municipal campsite was in fact a large grassy car park attached to a local community centre. They found themselves literally surrounded by cars and chatting locals all gathered for the Friday morning's senior education sessions.

"Bonjour, bonjour," they were dutifully greeted with as they tentatively emerged from the tent. But the locals couldn't disguise their obvious bemusement all the same.

Today however was different, the forecast was good, and 'glass half-full' Denis, was ready to go. With Maisie at his side what could possibly go wrong? Steady Denis.

Embarking from the early morning Brittany Ferries boat to Roscoff (other ferries are available, actually not from Plymouth) they had plenty of time to travel down to their first night's campsite in the Loire Atlantique. Unfortunately, Denis, as is his wont, had underestimated the amount of time it would take, or at least failed to consider just how long a four and half-hour drive, which turned out to be nearer six, is. Yes I know, Maisie couldn't believe it either!

Needing to avoid doing wrong turns with a sizeable trailer on the back, meant that by the time they were in striking distance of the campsite, the directions they took, required a little more precision, and things were getting a little fractious. Denis did indeed do a wrong turn which Maisie helpfully informed him of after he had committed to it. Denis then attempted to correct this by swinging around at a junction, which Maisie correctly predicted he wouldn't manage to get around. Denis then attempted to back the trailer, a thing that he had never done before, almost into a ditch, and then whilst failing to look for traffic coming the other way, proceeded to drive onto the wrong side of the road, a thing he usually did at least once a trip. Maisie screamed, Denis screeched and the rather large lorry rolled by.

"Hm, that was close." offered Denis, with some understatement.

Despite a couple more hiccoughs and several re-routes they eventually arrived safely at their destination, and it was still light!!

The campsite was lovely, empty and simple, but with very good facilities and very friendly owners. The camper was up in no time and they were soon settled down in the evening sunshine with a bottle of white and a bottle of red. The travails of the day soon forgotten.

"What's not to like?" thought Denis. "What's not to like?"

❖ ❖ ❖

They spent several very enjoyable days on the beautiful Atlantic coast close to the town of La Bernerie-en-Retz, just west of Nantes.

On the very first morning, Denis managed to realise his long-held intention of rising early and cycling into the local village boulangerie for a baguette and maybe a croissant or two, but it proved to be a slight disappointment when he discovered that the village was some distance away. On top of which, the folding 'his and her' boat bikes, that they had bought specifically for the trip, though Maisie was never very enthusiastic about, only had three gears and seemed not designed for anything but flat or downward slopes. On the way back he also had to struggle against the wind, whilst at the same time avoiding losing his La Baguette Parisienne and pains au chocolate. Still, Maisie, who hadn't even noticed he had gone, much appreciated his efforts, and more particularly, the pains au chocolate.

Denis never managed to tempt Maisie for an early morning trip down to the village, but they did enjoy several bicycle rides around the surrounding area, which was generally flat, during which they came across the impressive series of traditional carrelet fishing huts with their lift nets hanging over the coastal inlets.

"Eddie would have loved this." said Denis

Denis, who never expected a lot out of life, just a little now and then, had his own simple pleasures, one of which was his little oyster treat.

Having grown up as far away from the sea as is possible, Denis had come late to oysters but had always wanted to try them, and since first experiencing them on a day trip to Roscoff, he forever after always looked forward to this little indulgence. Of course, the coastline of the Loire Atlantique provided plenty of opportunities, and situated right on the beachfront, the curiously named, 'Les TonTons Nageurs Restaurant, offering a lovely assiette d'huîtres, 6 or 12, was the perfect place.

Maisie's general rule of thumb was seafood and don't eat it, and therefore her husband's enjoyment of these little bivalve molluscs was not shared or even understood by her, but she was happy to just let him get on with it.

However, on one occasion, whilst in the company of their friends Gloria and Eddie, who had emphatically declined Denis's invitation to try them, she made the mistake of remarking,

"Urgh, I don't know how you can eat those slimy things. No wonder they slip straight down your throat."

A comment she instantly regretted making.

"Well let me educate you on that one." Denis began.

"Actually, and this really irritates me, it is a common misconception that oysters are slimy. They are in fact anything but, and as to slipping straight down your throat, well that is nothing to do with being slippery. They, when opened, or 'shucked' as it is called, are still surrounded by the seawater in which they exist, and, as they are consumed, this water not only contributes to their unique authentic and natural taste, which evokes memories of the briny ocean but also helps to propel the little fellow, still alive, down into your stomach, where it can stay alive for up to fifteen minutes, apparently."

At that point, Gloria turned a strange grey colour and disappeared to the loos.

"Where's she going?" Denis said before continuing.

"It's the same with snakes, they're not at all slimy, but everyone thinks they are, well not everyone, obviously. But you know the thing that really irritates me even more? It's all those millions of oysters bought for Valentine's Day by people who haven't a clue how to open them and then they can't and so rather than shuck 'em, they chuck 'em, still alive!! It's like bloody pumpkins at Halloween, oh don't get me going on that."

"Oh for goodness sake Denis, calm down, it was only a comment. Just eat the bloody things."

Here in the sunshine, looking over the sea, he sat reverently admiring his freshly shucked Atlantic oysters, six juicy decent size 2s. Sitting in their own little pool of ocean and surrounding a little dish of lemon slices, and a bottle of Tabasco sauce.

"Mmm-mmm!"

Denis being Denis, only ever ate oysters whilst on holiday. It was his sound belief that oysters had to be eaten preferably outdoors, and whilst looking over the sea, accompanied by a glass of very cold white wine.

"Pretentious? Moi?" he would respond when challenged.

Making the most of the September sunshine, they enjoyed a couple of days picnicking on the long empty golden beaches, Maisie stretched out working on her tan whilst Denis enjoyed a swim in the sea.

"Come on Maisie, it's the warmest it gets all year." Denis called to his wife, trying to convince her to join him.

"What the hell does that even mean?" thought Maisie. "No thanks Denis." she called back, while at the same time turning over.

After a very enjoyable few days in the Loire d'Atlantique, including a day trip to the relative metropolis that is Pornic, and deciding they there were only so many oysters you could consume whilst staring across the briny ocean with a glass of very cold white wine, they decided to continue their journey south.

Back at the campsite, they were looking over the map and planning their next move. They considered heading down the coast towards La Rochelle, which they knew, and had enjoyed many times before, but felt that they should go somewhere they hadn't been, and decided on the region of the Limousin. Maisie was initially attracted merely by the fact that it was home to the famous cattle, which she remembered on the farm, as a child,

"Oh they are a lovely kind of reddy-brown colour Denis, and they have cute faces."

On that tenuous basis, they headed south for the Limousin.

◆ ◆ ◆

"It all sounds idyllic." she said, reading the guidebook as Denis drove.

"Do you know that the Limousin has the smallest population in mainland France?"

"Oh really." responded Denis, feeling ever so slightly usurped as the party's official historian.

"Hey, they reckon that the limousine car was named after it because all the residents of the Limousin wore huge hoods in winter and looked like big cars. Not sure about that one. No hold on, originally limousines, that's the car, had a big soft folding roof which resembled the Limousin residents' hooded cloaks. Or, the original limousine drivers donned large cloaks to protect them from the elements. Take your pick I suppose, eh Denis?"

"What? Yeh, whatever."

"You all right Denis?" enquired Maisie sweetly, enjoying her husband's irritation, before continuing.

"If you really want to get off the beaten track in France, head for the rural and little populated region of Limousin, suggests Theodore Bloom, that's who wrote the guide," she added helpfully.

"Discover medieval hilltop villages, imposing Chateaux and swathes of stunning scenery…." On reading 'hilltop villages' and 'stunning scenery', Maisie's voice began to slightly lose its cadence. Maisie was fine on the flat and could even cope with a little incline, as long as on both sides of the car, there was a very healthy portion of pavement.

The journey thus far from the Loire Atlantique, had been very smooth and mainly on the usual excellent, straight French roads, with very little traffic, and they were making excellent time. In fact, Denis had to keep reminding himself that he was pulling a sizeable trailer. However, having recently left the main D road, the last few miles had begun to give little indications of the 'rural bliss' referred to by Theodore, and as the roads began to take on an ever so slight incline and more curves, Maisie began to understand the significance of the description, 'hilltop villages'.

She continued to read to herself, and with a little more urgency....

"Slap bang in the centre of France, Limousin sits mostly atop the Massif Central, affording it lots of beautiful rolling hills, lush woodland, verdant river valleys, farmland as far as the eye can see, and even a bit of mountain...." Exuded Theo with palpable joy in his voice.

Maisie wasn't interested in his bloody lush, woodlands or his verdant rivers, the only things to strike her and were now dominating her thoughts, were the references to, 'massif central' and the 'mountain views'!

"Denis we are not going up a mountain are we? What did they say when you phoned them? Did they say they were up a mountain Denis, Denis!"

Denis, himself a little preoccupied with his emerging awareness of the trailer on the back, which was gradually becoming apparent in concert with the changing landscape, quickly framed a response.

"What, no of course not Maisie, look we aren't far off now."

Before carelessly adding, just as the car and trailer lurched around another bend and up and up,

"How bad can it get?"

To say that Maisie had never been a great lover of heights, and certainly not dizzy ones was to put it mildly. With the guide book now summarily despatched and sitting face-up on the back seat, with a smiling Theodore staring at the car ceiling, Maisie was concentrating very hard.

"Theodore could stick his lyrical musings where the sun don't shine." thought Maisie.

But at least now they were going down, oh no, now up and up again, oh and round and round. Just as Denis was beginning to have his own misgivings about 'Misty Havens Camping', the clue was in the name Denis mate, they emerged around a final tight bend and arrived apparently at the summit. Spread before them, running down from one of Theodore's beautiful rolling hills, was a huge green meadow and on it one solitary Motorhome, it was the campsite and the rest of the meadow, it seemed was theirs.

Set apart from the meadow was the residence of the owners, a fairly large rambling farmhouse surrounded by various farming artefacts from the days when it would have been a working farm. The couple did however have a thriving vegetable area and a sizeable menagerie of various breeds of chickens, ducks, an unusually friendly real goosey goosey gander, which farmer Maisie kept warning Denis not to get too close to, and a remarkable pure white peacock, which conscious of its unique plumage, strutted around with even more pride than usual.

The campsite was run by a typically friendly Dutch couple, Yannie and Suka who spoke perfect English,

"How do they do that?" thought Denis, "They all speak English!"

Welcoming them warmly, they confirmed that yes, the rest of the meadow was indeed theirs.

"Sun in the evening or sun in the morning?" they pondered.

"Evening!" they agreed.

The patron, Yannie, a very full of life character, informed

them that being a Saturday night and for a cost of 20 Euros a person, he would be providing a three-course gourmet meal with aperitifs, wine, and cheese, which they were very welcome to join himself and his other guests for. Before he managed to complete his invitation, Suka appeared to remind her husband that the English couple were already booked in. Yannie had just ruined Denis's surprise for Maisie, as he had booked it before they had set off that morning.

"Bloody typical!" he thought. "You try your best."

"Ah, that's really sweet Denis." said Maisie, which made him feel better.

Yannie did not disappoint, not only was he a great host, but he was also a very experienced trained chef, and the meal, a classic French creamy chicken main with a delicious Dutch take on a sticky toffee pudding, was magnificent.

Yannie theatrically introduced the meal with the starter.

"I give you this evening a classic Alsatian cheese tart!"

"Don't Denis." warned Maisie.

The delicious creamy and smoky cheese tart, which the guests devoured with a series of oohs and ahs, was a perfect start to some wonderful food.

Along with Suka and Yannie, Denis and Maisie were joined for the al fresco dining experience by five other couples, in fact, all of the residents of the campsite, which included those occupying several chalets hidden amongst the trees, and apart from Denis and Maisie, and one young French couple, they were all Dutch, but of course, all spoke English.

It didn't take long for Yannie to instigate some good-natured banter, mainly about English football, which Denis, after a few aperitifs, fended off and countered with his own banter. This led to Maisie having to remind him to be careful as they were guests, and more importantly, outnumbered. Though the evening and the food were faultless, it did contain a little bit of jeopardy in the form of several European hornets the size of house sparrows, which although continually flying in and out of the barn, fortunately, totally ignored the party below. Despite that, it still made Maisie a little nervous.

"Don't worry my love they're keeping to themselves and are probably harmless, big ones usually are."

Denis's comforting words were overheard by one of the guests who tactfully informed them that six people in France had died after being stung by them that year.

"Oh, nice. Another Kia, dear?" Denis suggested.

It proved to be a great evening and the slightly arduous journey had after all certainly been worth it. Lying in bed in their folding camper in the meadow, Denis suddenly said.

"Listen to that Maisie."

"What?" she said. "I can't hear anything."

"Exactly! Good night."

The previous day's discomfort, engendered mainly by the sudden change in the contours of the route, had greatly eased the next morning when the landscape turned out to be far less menacing than it had first appeared. The 'massif' as in 'massif central' had not necessarily related to the English word, or maybe it was just the foothills, and once the heavy trailer was removed from the car, the subsequent trips in and out of the campsite were pretty straightforward, in fact quite exhilarating, as like being on a huge roller coaster they wound up and down and round and round the roads leading from the campsite situated south of Limoges in the Parc Naturel Regional, Perigord-Limousin.

It didn't take them long to locate a decent supermarché for sustenance, and a lovely little, lac de loisir, for relaxation. On their day trips to the lake, Maisie parked herself under a tree and read, while Denis, like a child told to go and play, frolicked around in the waters of the empty lake. Every so often he would hide behind a wooden jetty, peeping out to see if Maisie had noticed him missing, and had begun to fret, but sadly, she never even noticed.

The days passed in tranquillity, the late September sun rose and set across their beautiful meadow, and early each morning Denis would walk up to the main block and pick up some freshly baked bread and croissants, also provided by chef Yannie. The boat bikes, being largely redundant in this fairly robust landscape, were barely used except when Denis having had enough relaxing, decided to venture off to the supermarché for the exercise. Maisie had warned him, that though it didn't seem that far in the car, should he really be cycling that distance?

"Well my love," he argued. "Why bother bringing the bikes if we don't use them?"

On the way back with the wind in his face and the majority of the slopes, so enjoyable on the outward journey, now being against him, he realised why.

After several days in their meadowland idyll, though they both felt they could stay longer, they decided to carry on. The late September sunshine was turning into a veritable Indian summer and so it was nice to have their decisions driven by choice rather than driving rain and they were still a long way from Jack's.

◆ ◆ ◆

Denis was keen to visit somewhere where they could make more use of their bikes. Maisie really wasn't that bothered, but as usual, indulged her excited husband, so they decided to head for Trebes on the Canal du Midi, famous for its cycling trails.

"They've got to be flat Maisie when you think about it, I mean, you know, canals."

"Yes Denis. Yes they would be." she said, barely remembering to respond.

"It's 240 kilometres long Maise."

"What is Denis?"

"Canal du Midi, originally named the Canal Royale en Languedoc and renamed by French revolutionaries to Canal du Midi in 1789. Cor! You can cycle all the way from Toulouse to Narbonne"

Maisie under-whelmed as usual by her husband's latest history lesson did have her ears pricked by the 240 kilometres.

"240 Kilometres! Don't get any ideas Denis!"

Denis was contented that there would be plenty of opportunities for cycling along the banks of the canal, the logistics of which could wait for now. In any case, as they ambled south along the fine straight roads towards Trebes, Denis's thoughts were a little pre-occupied with something he had spotted the previous evening whilst carefully planning the route. The ominously named, 'Black Mountains'.

"I've never heard of the bloody things," he thought, "when the hell did they pop up? Cor this could be fun, especially after the other day's performance."

Denis decided that there was no point prematurely freaking Maisie out, and anyway, she may well have fallen asleep by the time they reached them, and they probably weren't that bad. So he didn't tell her.

'Situated at the southern extremity of the Massif Central...' Denis had read. It went on to say...'The highest point of the Black Mountains at 1211 metres, The Nore Peak has a superb panoramic view from its orientation table you can see the Pyrènees, the Corbieres and even the Mediterranean Sea!'

"Bloody hell!" thought Denis. "The Mediterranean Sea! Maisie will be wetting herself with excitement. Well, she'll be wetting herself!"

"Why don't you have a little sleep my dear?" he suggested.

"No I'm enjoying the journey. Maisie answered. "The roads are so clear and the weather beautiful." she said, before adding.

"Mind you it does look as if it is getting a bit black in the distance. Are they clouds?"

"Hmm." thought Denis nervously.

It was the case that far away on the horizon where the long stretch of road seemed to disappear, black clouds were ominously gathered.

"At least they are shrouding the Black Mountains." thought Denis, trying to be positive.

A while later, just like getting onto an escalator before you're quite expecting it, the car seemed to suddenly jerk upwards and disappeared into what indeed proved to be a dark mist as it began its ascent of the Black Mountains, what had appeared to have been black clouds obviously were. The density of the pine trees which provided the 'black' in the Black Mountains, added to the gloom.

"Whoa, what happened there Denis?" enquired a slightly shaken Maisie.

"Are we climbing Denis?" his wife's agitation intensifying with the question.

"Denis!"

"Er it's erm, yes er." responded Denis, before mumbling pathetically something about there may be some hills between here and Trebes.

But as the angle of the car began to sharpen, Denis was aware that Maisie's agitation was reaching a new and dangerous level.

"Don't worry yourself Maisie love, we can't be far off," he found himself repeating. "once we get to the top of this bit it'll be fine."

And it probably would have been if it hadn't been for the roadworks.

Dropping down into a lower gear, the car despite the heavy trailer was happily coping with the steepness of the climb. But then around a bend, flashing lights signalled the approach of roadworks and temporary traffic lights.

"Roadworks and traffic lights on a bloody mountain!?" groaned a frustrated Denis, rather carelessly.

"Mountain? What mountain!?" responded Maisie, the panic rising in her voice.

"Oh gawd, you know Maisie, hills, you know slightly bigger ones."

"We're going up a mountain aren't we Denis, we're going up a bloody mountain!! A bloody mountain! Oh shit, shit, shit!"

But Denis didn't have time to respond. At that moment the car ground to a halt in front of a smiling workman in his high viz jacket, raising his hand with a flourish, just in case the driver hadn't noticed the red light.

"Bloody hell!" thought Denis, as he felt the car jerk back slightly in response to the weight of the trailer, which by now was at an extremely oblique angle to horizontal. In happier circumstances, Denis might have remarked on the magnificence of the view, but he decided not to.

After what seemed like an age, the light turned green.

"Thank God for that." thought Denis, mightily relieved until on negotiating another bend, they were confronted with another red light.

"You are kidding me!" he groaned.

As he had pulled away from the first set of lights, Denis had been frustrated that the car did not want to go into third gear. As he pulled away from the second set, he was becoming aware that the car was actually beginning to struggle just a little. By the time they were pulling through the fourth set, he was permanently stuck in first gear, his temperature gauge indicated serious overheating, and a definite smell of burning was becoming evident.

Maisie by this time had her head buried in her lap, and was rocking back and forth. By the time the temperature gauge was vertical and had nowhere else to go; Denis still stuck in first, and also with nowhere else to go, resorted to his 'Oh Jesus prayer', which was simply just that.

"Oh Jesus!" he offered up in sincere supplication.

At that moment, apart from the view which was indeed magnificent, though he still couldn't quite make out the Mediterranean sea through the pine trees, the car seemed to level up, Denis managed to slip into second and the temperature gauge began to gradually begin its descent back to normal. They were going down. Down, down and more down. Eventually, still not quite able to exhale his breath, they emerged into the sunshine on the other side.

"Thank you God, oh thank you God." Denis burst out.

A traumatised Maisie sat staring straight ahead, whimpering.

It was never really mentioned again at least not for several years and it never became one of those things,

"We will laugh about it in years to come."

After emerging from the Black Mountains, the road mercifully continued straight and relatively flat, ensuring that Maisie's equilibrium slowly but surely began to be restored. Fortunately for Denis, his dear wife's transition from calm to hysteria, to calm, could be relatively swift and on this occasion, it was further aided by their arrival at the campsite.

Situated in the village of Rustiques, a short drive from the medieval town of Trebes, it was spacious with well-appointed camping spaces, and also boasted a beautiful pool, and magnificent views across the plain to the ancient walled town of Carcassonne, a mere 7km to the east. The campsite, which was refreshingly open, provided a much-needed antidote to their previous incarceration in the dense pine forests of the Black Mountains. There was also a large community area with a bar and restaurant, however as they had begun to notice as the journey had progressed, the tourist season was beginning to close down and so neither the bar nor the restaurant were fully open.

What was prominent in reception, and spotted immediately by Denis, was a poster from the local history society that advertised a free walking tour of the local area beginning on Tuesday from reception at 10 am.

"Brilliant!" thought Denis. "A couple of days for Maisie to get back to normal, and then I'm sure she'll be up for it."

Apparently, though obviously dwarfed by its near neighbour of Carcassonne, Rustiques with its population of only 530 souls, was steeped in its own history dating back to the 5th century, when in response to barbarian invasions by the Visigoths, Sarrasins and Francs, the locals united for safety on the surrounding high ground, from which they could spot invaders.

"Bloody fascinating round here Maisie." said Denis, now back in the camper and in the process of convincing his wife that the tour would be great, and it was only for 90 minutes. Happily for Denis, Maisie was on her second gin and tonic and agreed without putting up too much of a struggle.

On enquiring about the tour in perfect French, the friendly chap behind the reception immediately informed Denis, that bottles of beer were actually available from the fridge, along with an honesty box. Trying again, with a bit more perfect French, the receptionist went on to tell Denis that there was no need to book, just turn up and that the tour guide actually spoke German.

"We're English." said Denis.

"Oh yes." came the reply, and an apology.

"He speaks English too," before adding, for no apparent reason, "and also some Spanish."

When they arrived at reception at 10am prompt the next morning, there were already two other couples there, both German and looking a little impatient. Within five minutes or so, a gentleman of senior years, armed with a clipboard and bunch of papers turned up and introduced himself as Claud, their tour guide, and an ancestor of the original Château inhabitants.

By the time Claud finished his welcome and preamble about the history of the history society in German and English, their numbers had been swollen along the way by various new participants joining the group, all French. By the time they were ready to move off after Claud had repeated his welcome in French, there were seventeen in the party.

The tour was indeed very informative, and Claud's delivery of the script generally relaxing, and an easy listen. The slight problem, which Maisie had observed shortly into his preamble, was the time it was taking for their enthusiastic host to proudly translate it into three languages. This slight hiccough was eased somewhat when, much to Denis's chagrin, one of the Germans told Claud that there was no need to translate it into German, as they understood English.

Unfortunately, this only encouraged Denis to develop further a competition, which had been brewing between himself and the same German fellow, as to who could ask Claud the most impressive questions, which Claud gladly entertained. The two adversaries ended up resembling a pair of bidders at an auction, each one glancing over at the other to try to anticipate their next move, which went on until their respective wives had had enough and put a stop to it.

Despite the enthusiasm, and genuine interest at the start, by the time an hour was up, Claud's mellifluous tone was beginning to take effect on his audience, and the attention of some of the company began to drift. Before too long a few yawns and discreet glances at watches became apparent.

Shortly afterwards, with his back to the group and his attention focussed on the latest fact, or artefact that he was explaining, some of Claud's group seized the opportunity to quietly slip away. Claud, thoroughly immersed in the sharing of his obvious passion, hadn't really noticed until all that was left were Denis, Maisie, and the four punctilious Germans, who, spot on 90 minutes, graciously thanked their host, and promptly departed, leaving just Denis and Maisie.

Not really taking the hint, Claud continued for another twenty minutes until they had completed the circuit back to the campsite reception, whereupon, after profusely thanking Claud, Maisie quickly disappeared back to the trailer to sleep for the afternoon, and Denis headed for the fridge.

Weather-wise, the next day looked particularly promising and the perfect day to cycle along the Midi Canal, which whilst on its way from Toulouse to Narbonne, passed right through Trebes. With the route from the campsite to Trebes being rather undulating in places, Denis not wanting Maisie to be put off before they set off, prudently decided to drive to the canal, so with the folding bikes stashed into the boot of the car, they headed off. Within twenty minutes they were positioned on the cycle track at the side of the canal ready to go.

Denis was in high spirits. He already liked Trebes, mainly because the previous evening having driven down to explore, they had discovered a lovely restaurant where the proprietress was not only really friendly, but also indulged Denis, in conducting the whole exercise in French, and they had even been served with what they thought Denis had asked for!! Some achievement.

The sun continued to shine down on them as they set off. Naturally, the cycle track running right along the side of the canal was nice and flat. Trebes, being a bit of a hub, and launch point for Carcassonne, was a busy place that morning and this particular stretch of the canal was adorned with a variety of barges and canal boats, some uniform looking obviously for hire, and lots more of various shapes and sizes, from modest to luxury.

"Wouldn't you love to do that Maisie?"

"Well yes, the bit where you sit on the deck in the sunshine sipping Prosecco, but I wouldn't fancy the effort involved, what about all those gates you have to go through?"

"Locks my love." muttered Denis, realising that convincing Maisie of the joys of canal boating could wait for another day.

The cycle track, not being paved, had quite a few rough bits and potholes, so they had to pay attention, they were, however, making very good progress. They were headed to a village about six kilometres away, where Denis pictured stopping for a light lunch, maybe a glass of wine and a croque-monsieur. Now and again they would stop to watch the boaters with various degrees of competency, negotiate around the confined space afforded by the locks. The number of locks they encountered on the relatively short journey surprised Denis, and he too was beginning to wonder if he could 'be arsed' with all that.

One particular canal boat captain, bedecked appropriately in all the regalia of a seasoned practitioner, seemed to respond to his latest audience. While his wife and two children, paying little attention, indulged in their al fresco lunch, he, having noticed the pair of curious onlookers, continued to carry out his task with an added flourish. As the lock slowly filled with water, he expertly manoeuvred his vessel around the tightness of the space, in readiness to pilot it through the lock gate as soon as it opened. Unfortunately, vainly feeling the need to entertain his audience with his skills just one more time, he unnecessarily swung the bow of the boat around a little too hard and sent the pristine front of the vessel into the side of the lock wall.

"Whoops!" said Denis, rather too loudly, prompting Maisie to signal it was time to leave.

And so before the embarrassed Captain could blame anyone but himself, Denis and Maisie were off. Fading into the distance they could hear the sound of the screaming voice of his angry wife, whose lunch, including her liquid refreshment, he had propelled clean off the boat and into the canal.

Sadly, as they continued along the pathway, they noticed that most of the establishments along the route were closed, and the track, up to now sticking closely to the canal, was suddenly taking them off the path and literally across a farmer's field before reuniting with the canal quite a distance further on.

They were both feeling a little bit jaded, and by the time they reached the village, their mood didn't improve when they realised that being a Monday, everything was shut! About to face the full impact of his wife's frustration, Denis noticed just up an adjacent leafy lane, a little sign handwritten on a piece of card, which read,

'Vin ici.' accompanied by a smiley face.

The rough-looking signage at the end of a pathway leading to a house didn't look too promising, but after gaining the attention of the owner, who greeted them with the kind of enthusiasm Denis believed could only be found in France, they were soon seated under a shady little tree, accompanied by glasses of vin, rouge et blanc. The hostess couldn't have been more friendly.

"This is the life eh Maisie? I told you the bikes were a good idea." said Denis.

Maisie was reserving her judgement, they still had to cycle back.

"Should we have another one." enquired Denis.

"Do you think that's wise on bikes?" replied Maisie.

"No." said Denis.

"OK." replied Maisie, and so they did.

The journey back proved a little more challenging. It had become somewhat overcast, and the wind, though not very strong, on their backs on the outward journey and therefore helping to propel them along, was now in their faces.

"Why does it always do that to me?" demanded a frustrated Denis. "Bloody wind!"

The six kilometres they had covered in the sunshine had not seemed too bad, but the six back on their bikes with little wheels and the choice of only three gears were more of a challenge than a pleasure.

Denis was relieved with his decision to bring the car down to the canal, cycling back to the campsite may have proven a pedal too far. Begrudgingly, along with Maisie, he was beginning to realise the limitations of deck bikes.

"Maybe they are only designed to ride around decks." he thought.

It had overall, been an enjoyable day, though Denis realised that as usual, he had probably pushed his wife's indulgence a little too far, and it was indeed, a while before the bikes got another airing.

By the time they had returned from the exertions of their cycle ride, they were ready to try out for the first time, the beautiful pool. Unfortunately, despite Denis's belief that the sea was always at its warmest at the back-end of the year, it obviously didn't apply to swimming pools, which though by now the late afternoon sun was shining down on, was freezing.

"Whoa!" gasped Maisie as she enthusiastically plunged in. "I wasn't expecting that. You could have warned me Denis."

But the slightly asthmatic Denis was struggling to breathe, never mind speak. After a quick length of the pool they sat at the side wrapped in their towels looking over into the distance, where astride the skyline, they could see the distinct profile of the famous walled city of Carcassonne. With the sun setting behind it, it was an impressive sight. While Maisie stretched herself out on a sun bed attempting to extract the final rays of the afternoon sunshine, Denis sat at the side of the pool contemplating the magnificence of the Citée in the distance.

"That's tomorrow's little jaunt." promised Denis. "Do you know Maisie, it used to be right on the border with Spain but then they moved it, the border that is, and so it wasn't really doing much and it fell into disrepair and was going to be demolished, but the locals kicked up a big fuss and some famous French architect had it restored in 1844. Do you know that it is not just a castle, it's actually a town within the walls, and has over a thousand residents!" Denis, sensing silence, turned around to find that Maisie, having already departed, was not in fact there.

"Do you know, I wish you wouldn't keep doing that." he moaned. "It's so bloody annoying!"

The next day they drove the short distance into the town of Carcassonne, which over the centuries had grown up around the famous citadel. The closer they got, the more impressive the castle and its surrounding fortifications appeared. Maisie, who had been a little dubious about Denis and his description of it, was instantly impressed and was actually getting quite excited. In a splendidly organised fashion, a little bavette ran from the town car park to the gates of the citadel high up on the hill, its huge structure scrutinising the surrounding area like a giant sentinel. What had looked impressive from a distance, was truly magnificent up close.

"Wow!!" Was about all they could say. Maisie couldn't wait.

But before setting off on the bavette, Denis couldn't resist a stroll around the Saturday morning market. It was particularly impressive, and being close to Spain, was more diverse than usual in the variety of its stalls. Breads, cheeses, fresh fish, anti-pasta, regional sausages, meats, wonderfully smelling rotisseries full of dripping Farmer's Chickens, stalls and stalls, full of beautiful fresh vegetables and fruits. Denis never ceased to be amazed at the huge array of products available at French markets, though at the same time he always found it all rather overwhelming, and rarely ended up buying very much, anyway they could hardly carry it around with them all day, so he settled on some huge juicy peaches and some pastries.

After a short climb on the bavette, they stood before the magnificence of ancient Carcassonne, and what appeared to be exciting from the outside did not disappoint on the inside. It was like all the little market towns that Maisie had ever visited, all rolled into one huge attraction. With its endless maze of streets, which you could get lost in but then soon find your way out again. It's countless bars and restaurants, curio shops, craft shops, bakeries and pâtisseries, it was literally, right up Maisie's street. Though the walled town was essentially geared for tourists, it was refreshingly not excessively so. Prices were generally reasonable, food and drink excellent, and overall it provided a brilliant visit.

"Gloria and Eddie would have loved this Denis, well Gloria would." Thinking of how much fun she and her friend could have had wandering around this place together.

And indeed it was a real treat. In fact, they returned the following day, and even the day after that in order to take in a very satisfying al fresco meal under the shade of wisteria-draped pergola. The final visit inevitably included, as any trip with Denis would, a guided tour of the ancient castle buildings, ramparts and Cathedral, which Denis had had his eye on from the start, and which even Maisie, high on Carcassonne vapours, had to admit was pretty interesting and enjoyable, especially the free concert of atmospheric 'a cappella' choral singing they were treated to in the splendid surroundings of the 12th-century basilica.

"Ooh it gave me goosebumps that did Denis." admitted Maisie.

After finishing the tour, they searched out the little restaurant they had booked for lunch and ended their visit with a lovely meal at which Denis got to try out the famous, 'cassoulet', which seemed to be for sale, though expensively, in most of the shops.

Denis, once having been subjected somewhere in mid-France, to the rather questionable delights of a plateful of 'local cuisine' which had turned up on his plate as a barely edible dollop of overdone wallpaper paste, had ever since harboured a bit of a grudge when it came to, 'local dishes'. (Don't mention the andouille!!) Especially food that had begun life as poor people's food, but had for commercial reasons been elevated to cult status. To be fair, he loved his Hungarian goulash as much as the next man, but at the end of the day, it was, "only stew with loads of paprika in it."

"It's all just like Lancashire hot pot and Irish stew, simple and filling but nothing mysterious. They're even trying to turn bloody black pudding into some kind of exotic niche food."

For Denis, cassoulet fitted this perception perfectly. Originating from South-west France, it was the food of peasants, a simple assemblage of what ingredients were available with beans thrown in. It appeared however that, culturally at least, the plateful in front of Denis had travelled a long way since then.

The first cassoulet is claimed by the city of Castelnaudary which maintains that the dish somehow helped defeat an English siege of the town during the Hundred Years War which, understandably, helped to propel its cult status. It is also the feature of competitions across the region, with each town believing that they make the one true cassoulet, even arguing about which type of bean should be used. There is a brotherhood – the Grande Confrerie du Cassoulet and even an Académie

Universelle du Cassoulet.

However despite its 'unique' French identity, the word 'cassoulet' is cognate with the Spanish word 'cazoleta' and Catalan 'casslolet', but best not to share that with the French.

Yes, along with, driving down the middle of country roads, Associations, indignation, peeing at the side of the road, endless bizous and having to weigh your tomatoes before going to the checkout, the dish which Denis was about to sample was right up there with the most immutable and revered aspects of French culture and it was why Denis just loved France. Tuck in Denis.

As the first spoonful landed in his mouth, Denis delivered his verdict…..

"Hm, bean stew." he pronounced, rather dismissively.

"Denis!!"

Back at the camper that evening, Maisie, having had a wonderful day was presently, glass in hand, bathing in the balm of its recollection. Denis observing the glow emanating from his dear wife seized his opportunity.

He had discovered with amazement, a few days earlier, that the Catalan Dragons, a Perpignan-based rugby team in the English league, were playing his team in the last game of the season.

"Er, hmm, tomorrow my love, I wondered if you fancied moving on a bit further South and East to, er, Perpignan? Yeh it's, erm, a town across the Roussillon plane at the, er, foot of the er, Pyrènees."

Reflecting later on how things had unfolded Denis concluded that it was more likely the word Pyrènees, rather than the hesitancy in his voice, caused by his little bit of subterfuge, that had triggered it, but it was hard to tell. What Denis hadn't found hard to recognise, was the significance of Maisie's reaction. Bursting into tears and with a level of hysteria he had not witnessed since he had once thrown a live chicken on her bed whilst camping in Northumberland. She rocked back and forth crying,

"I just want to go to Jack's, I want to go to Jack's."

"Cor blimey." he thought. "She's still suffering PTSD from the Black Mountains!!"

◆ ◆ ◆

The next day they headed West.

Reassuring Maisie that the route West was flatter than a flat road in Holland, well he hoped it was, he managed to convince her that the distance from the campsite to Pau was too far to do in one day. She was therefore happy to agree to one more stop along the way, though she did have more than the usual input into the location of their final campsite. Several hours later, after a stress-free drive, they rolled into a campsite just outside the town of Plaisance, Northeast of Pau.

Their arrival at what appeared to be the campsite equivalent of the 'Marie Celeste', confirmed that the tourist season was well and truly closing down. Having taken the best part of half an hour to track down anyone resembling a receptionist, which happened to be a leftover guest from a wedding hosted by the campsite the previous day, who managed to hail a real receptionist. They were finally booked in, and once again, as soon as the last of the wedding guests had departed, had the whole place to themselves.

Shortly after their arrival, Denis thought that he may have died and gone to heaven, when the very helpful wedding guest, another larger-than-life Dutch man who of course spoke English, enthusiastically told Denis that there was a whole keg of Leffe beer left over from the wedding, which he wondered if Denis would like to help him finish. Sadly, after furnishing Denis with just one pint, the larger-than-life Dutchman disappeared along with the Leffe, and Denis never saw either of them again.

Sloping back to the camper, Denis wondered if he had misunderstood him.

"You all right Denis?" enquired Maisie, who always knew when he wasn't.

"Yeh, its just that, you know that big guy, the chatty one?"

"You mean the man from the Netherlands, the friendly one? He seemed really nice, didn't he?"

"A bit over-friendly if you ask me."

"Oh and what about it?"

"Nothing." Denis replied.

Despite itching to get on now that their ultimate goal was in sight, the continuing beautiful weather proved difficult to resist and so they enjoyed several more days of camping in the autumn sunshine. The presence of a very nice restaurant just over the road from the campsite, which served a reasonably priced buffet style plat de jour, was a real draw, as was the campsite's deserted swimming pool.

Appearing to have been the result of an attempt to create

a regular-shaped pool, which had been abandoned halfway through, and the resultant hole in the ground simply lined and filled with water, the pool was both very aesthetic in shape and attractive in appearance. The very bright blue lining, sloping gently down into the deeper middle, affording opportunities for both swimming and dabbling. However with the autumn sunshine its only source of heat, it was freezing, but nice to sit around with a book, which Maisie mainly did, but Denis being Denis didn't like to 'waste' it, so he took the plunge on more than one occasion, and even talked Maisie into trying it out once, but only once.

The town of Plaisance, rather sad and abandoned looking, was only a short cycle away, so they enjoyed several evenings in the town square, enjoying a sundowner and also visited the market, which in stark contrast to Carcassonne, was also rather sparse and abandoned looking. Denis feeling a bit sorry for one forlorn-looking lady selling just tomatoes, of which she didn't even have many of those, asked for two, "s'il vous plait". Which the lady handed to Denis and requested two Euros! Which Denis duly paid, as you do, and walked away muttering under his breath,

"Bloody hell, two Euros for two bloody tomatoes, bloody hell! Why didn't I say something?"

It did prompt him, shortly afterwards, to look up and learn how to say,

"Tu te marres n'est-pas?!"

Which roughly translated as 'you're 'avin a laugh aint ya??'

A phrase, which on future jaunts through France, he delighted in making use of several times, and which despite Maisie's 'health warning', often provided Denis with a very satisfying response.

The slight change in the weather and that inescapably itchy feel brought by knowing it's nearly time to leave, prompted them to strike camp for the last time and head for Jack's. Despite Maisie's previous keenness to get there, departure day was tinged with very mixed emotions, it was after all the end of another chapter and a very enjoyable one at that. With the help of his dear wife, Denis had successfully realised his latest venture.

He and Maisie, had finally meandered their way down, 'La Belle France'.

◆ ◆ ◆

Denis, though still encrusted in his icy tomb, was beginning to ever so slightly warm up and begin to show signs of life. His recollections were becoming less distanced and more vivid but, of course, he still had a silly grin on his face as he recalled.......

CHAPTER 6

Plouneour-Trez! Ah yes Plouneour-Trez, now there's a memory thought Denis, a faint smile appearing on his face as he settled back once again into his snowy cocoon.

◆ ◆ ◆

It had been some journey, arriving in the dark after a four-hour trek from Caen.

Due to the limited nature of the winter timetable, the relatively simple ferry trip from Plymouth to Roscoff had on this occasion not been an option. Instead, it had meant a six-hour ferry journey from Portsmouth, departing at 8.15 am. This necessitated leaving Plymouth at some un-Godly hour, to ensure that they arrived at the ferry port in good time. The brief respite presented by the possibility of a shorter crossing to St Malo, had at the last minute, been mysteriously cancelled. Consequently, after being en route for around eighteen hours, by the time they had finally arrived late at night at the cottage, which would be their home for the next two months, they were certainly relieved but a little, let's say, rough around the edges.

Overall, the journey had been relatively straightforward. Maisie's assistance ensured that Denis had once again quickly adjusted to being on the 'wrong' side of the road, and though distracted ever so slightly by the magical site of the frost-bedecked flora, that appeared every so often on the verge of the A84, they had made good time. It was only the last part of the journey, when the self-assured, almost cocky voice of the Satnav, suddenly seemed to betray an element of doubt, that Denis who, along with the equally infuriating Alexa, famously allowed himself to become exercised by the "bloody stupid thing" began to lose his cool.

Maisie, seeming to ignore the fact that they appeared to be just about to enter a farmer's field, attempted to reassure him.

"For goodness sake Denis, calm down! Look we can't be far off. Just pull over and let's take stock."

"Stupid bloody Satnav!" muttered her husband.

After making a few adjustments they managed to realign Jane the Satnav, and despite his cynicism, Denis had to admit that without her guidance they would never have reached their destination, a petit cottage nestled in the bowels of the ancient Breton settlement of Plouneour-'Traezh'.

Several weeks previously, in another of his not uncommon moments of inspiration, Denis had decided that spending a couple of winter months in Brittany, in a little garret, as he saw it, would be a good idea, relatively cheap and also rather romantic. With a small 'r'.

"Situated in the department of Finisterre, in the extreme west of Brittany, Plouneour-Trez, lies 37 kilometres North of the port town of Brest, the most populous town in the region, though not the capital. That honour rests with Quimper, another even more ancient town which was originally settled during Roman times and was the ancient capital of Cornouaille, Brittany's most traditional region, and has a distinctive Breton-Celtic character, Quimper not Brest. Am I boring you Maisie?"

"Sorry Denis, what were you saying?"

"Moron." muttered Denis, "I will continue. Actually I won't, just to show you."

"Sorry Denis, what was that?"

Both Denis and Maisie had many happy memories of previous times in Brittany, having holidayed numerous times when Clare and Jack were young. Often accompanied by their close friends Eddie and Gloria and on one occasion by Gloria's Dad, Maurice, affectionately known as Granddad.

"Oh happy days." recalled Denis. "We had some adventures eh? Blimey, you wouldn't believe the half of it!!"

Denis had been to Brest only on one occasion in the past. The trip had been prompted by an attempt to improve his French, and involved, sour milk, lost teeth and a disastrous stay with, of all people, an Ambassador with the impressive brief to develop and enhance relationships between Brittany and the UK, which he spectacularly failed to achieve. But that really was another story.

Denis's first day back in his beloved France was everything he had hoped. It began on a very positive note when he was woken up by the sunshine streaming through the window.

"South facing! Boom boom!! Boom boom Mavis, South facing. Yes!!!"

"Really Denis?" groaned a comatose Maisie. "What time is it?"

"Er, 8.30-ish my love, 7.30 in old money." he added under his breath.

"Denis."

Stepping outside to survey their accommodation, Denis was

more than happy to find that with the benefit of broad daylight, the impression formed the previous night in the pitch dark, was not significantly different.

"Ooh medieval." mused Denis, "How romantic." (Oh come on Denis!)

Dwarfed by the huge edifice of the Eglise Saint-Pierre de Plouneour-Trez, the cottage, resplendent in Breton blue and complete with newly renovated shutters, stood on the corner of a long sloping bend, which seemed to wind downward and into another era. At the bottom of the slope and reinforcing the impression of ancient times, stood a magnificently restored, 'Maison De Lavage', where ancient wives gathered to launder ancient clothes for their ancient lazy bastard husbands.

"Wow!" thought Denis, "Wow!"

As he stood there in contemplation, a young girl accompanied by a scruffy little dog on a lead appeared around the corner. Desperate to greet his first encounter with a local, Denis hesitated because sadly, 'strange' men did not naturally speak to little girls anymore in case the greeting was misunderstood. But before he could resolve his dilemma the little girl called out

"Bonjour monsieur."

"How refreshing. How French." thought Denis.

"Bonjour, bonjour!" responded Denis, perhaps with a little too much enthusiasm, before skipping back inside to help his dear wife out of bed with a welcome cup of coffee.

Denis's joy was further reinforced, when he discovered that there was a Lidl store (other Supermarchés are available), just fourteen minutes' drive away. As much as one of the attractions of Brittany was its local foods, Denis also loved a bargain and even in the relatively expensive France, Lidl still provided it.

Their first excursion to Lidl also provided the stage on which Denis experienced the first French drama of this particular trip.

A little over gassed by the apparent success of his command of French on negotiating passport control on their arrival in France, which had hardly stretched him. His response to discovering that his trolley token didn't fit in the Lidl trolleys was to casually stride over to the checkout before breezing past the queue of shoppers and confidently asking the young lady at the till if she might have a 'jeton de chariot' because this one 'marche pas.'

All good so far.

The young lady responded positively, and with a broad smile, graciously handed Denis a little blue coin. Equally graciously, Denis thanked her and returned the smile, which, on noticing the ripple of French indignation on the faces of the people in the queue, caused by his jumping it, broadened ever so slightly.

At this point, things began to fall apart a little.

Initially, Denis, when he had discovered, that his own token didn't fit, had decided that as they weren't buying very much, he would forgo a trolley. However on noticing a bottle of Cote de Rhone Village, at just over two euros and thinking he might treat himself to a couple, quickly changed his mind about the trolley and on the way to get the token, picked a bottle up as he went past.

Unfortunately therefore, as he walked away from the checkout to go outside for the trolley, he still had the bottle of wine in his hand.

"Er, excusez-moi, monsieur." called over the young lady, and then something Denis didn't quite catch.

One of the flaws in Denis's command of the French language was that in order to deal with specific situations, his intended deliveries were often very much planned and rehearsed, and so when confronted with a stream of the unexpected, he often became intimidated, and things could often rapidly collapse. Happily, on this occasion, Denis, realising the cause of the girl's concern, quickly recovered his equilibrium and smiling once again, returned back into the body of the shop and replaced the bottle on the shelf, before going outside for the trolley. All was again fine until now finding himself closer to the entrance door than the checkout, he decided rather than going back through the checkout he would wait until someone was entering and slip out that way, which he did, immediately setting off the alarm.

Eventually, rather sheepishly, and running the gauntlet of an increasingly bemused checkout girl, and a string of seriously indignant customers, a by now rather more ruffled Denis, managed to get himself outside and back in with a trolley.

"That you setting off the alarm Denis?" Maisie enquired casually, as he finally caught up with her.

"How does she always bloody know these things?"

◆ ◆ ◆

Plouneour -Trez, 'a sleepy little town somewhere in Brittany', was indeed little and very sleepy.

It is a fact that when passing through many towns and villages in France the question that often arises is,

"Does anyone actually live here?"

Plouneour -Trez was no different.

Apart from its imposing Church of St Peter, the only other premises of note were a café, which also served as the official boulangerie. Official because every village in France must have a bakery. (It's a French Revolution thing.) A bar, another café and a grocery store called Breizh Market. 'Breihz' being Breton for Bretagne. And that is it. It seemed that most things in the area were seasonal and when Denis and Maisie arrived in January, Plouneour-Trez had been well and truly, 'seasonalised.'

"Yes, apparently Maisie, since the French Revolution, every village in France has to have a boulangerie selling bread. Because, apparently, Marie Antoinette had famously told the peasants that they should eat cake if they had no bread, actually I think she meant brioche, but that's no better really, anyway, whichever, at the time it had not gone down too well. Literally, I suppose." he chuckled to himself.

"Also if there is no bakery in the village, a storehouse or even the post office, will display a 'depot de pain' sign, signifying that bread is brought in and sold from there. Amazing eh Maise?"

 Maisie was not usually responsive to Denis's rambling tutorials, but on this occasion, her attention had been sparked by the mention of, 'boulangerie', which she associated with, 'pâtisserie', which lead seamlessly to, 'pâtisseries', which immediately sent Maisie into paroxysms of, 'ecstasies'. Maisie was generally steadfast and rational, but stand her in front of a shop window full of French pâtisseries with the hint of a possible purchase, and she was gone.

"Cor blimey it says that even the ingredients of the baguette are defined by law! They can only be made from four ingredients: wheat, flour, water, salt and yeast, and, apart from the 'depots', they must be made on the premises that they are sold."

"Hold on that's five? Is salt an ingredient Maisie?"

"Yes."

"What about water?"

"Can you leave any of them out Denis?"

"Er, not really."

"Then they are all ingredients Denis."

"Wow, even the holidaying of Parisienne bakers is legislated! They have to go on vacation in bloody shifts so there is always plenty around producing bread during July and August!"

Maisie's lack of response to this latest soupçon of information led Denis to suspect that her sense of ecstasy was beginning to wane a little, and so though carrying on with his fascinating discoveries, he now kept them to himself.

And anyway it was time to experience their first little bit of indulgence, a trip to a crêperie.

"Now, you are talking Denis!"

In times past, Denis and Maisie's transport around Brittany and indeed France, was very much reliant on four wheels, or two feet, though they did once complete a famous cycle trip from

Roscoff to Hanvec to stay in a rustic 'woodland gite'. A journey which had involved fifty-eight kilometres of varying terrain, some rather challenging.

That trip had been with friends other than Eddie and Gloria, who unfortunately had been ruled out because Gloria couldn't ride a bike.

They were accompanied on that particular occasion by their good friends, Mikos Mikanos, who Denis referred to as, 'Phil the Greek", because, as his name would suggest, he was originally from Greece, and his beautiful wife, the curiously named Delphinium. Delphinium hailed from some South-Sea island and often sported a frangipani blossom in her hair, and could always be relied upon to perform a hula hula dance in a grass skirt, whenever a social function demanded it.

By presenting them with a globe to illustrate the route, Denis had convinced Jack and Clare, that the trip from Roscoff in the North of Brittany, to Hanvec in the South, was all downhill. And so some four hours after leaving the Port of Roscoff, the party of Denis, 'Phil the Greek,' Clare and Jack, finally arrived in Hanvec. Bringing up the rear, safely in the backup vehicle, provided by "I ain't cycling!" Maisie, were Maisie, Delphinium and the two young Mikanos boys, George and Adi.

Despite the arduous journey, the intrepid cyclists arrived none the worse for wear, except for Jack, who sported two rather swollen 'items' that were the result of constant contact with his saddle. Maisie was stricken with guilt for her poor baby, while Jack, though coping well enough with his new grapefruits, which happily began to return to normal as the days passed, struggled with his mother's less than discreet outpourings of sympathy.

Thanks to Mikos, with his expertise in forest skills, and

Delphinium with her wonderful cooking, all in all, they had enjoyed a wonderful week and it had been a great trip.

Happy memories of times past.

Years later, cycling still wasn't on Maisie's list of hobbies, in fact Maisie, apart from on flat canal paths, did not do cycling. That was until a recent holiday in Greece, of all places when on the way back from a holiday island they stopped over in Athens and Denis impulsively booked an electric bike tour of the ancient city. Well it seemed a good idea at the time, but after booking it, it did occur to him that he had neglected to factor Maisie into the equation, still, he could work on that later.

The first response was not too promising. You can imagine,

"Denis I am not riding a bike around the hills of Athens in 30-degree heat! No!"

However, although Maisie had spent much of her married life kicking and screaming down the routes of Denis's madcap schemes, in fact, much of the time she was the one making them work. And so eventually with the promise of a meal out in the trendy Plaka area of Athens, and with the tenuous linking of a performance of a cultural show, high on Acropolis hill, which had actually nothing to do with the bike ride, she gave in.

And boy did she give in!

For months after, beginning with Gloria, everybody she met was treated to an account of Maisie's electric bike adventure. She was smitten to the point that as soon as they had returned home, they began their research, and shortly after, Denis and Maisie were the proud owners of their own TREK Verve 1 electric bikes. (other makes are available). And better still they had brought them on their trip to Brittany!

Despite Maisie's miraculous conversion, Denis still had a little work to do convincing Maisie that her adventure in Athens could be repeated in France. Maisie did not generally do any driving in France and cycling on the wrong side of the road did not appeal to her either. However she did know that the roads were generally less busy, and after Denis had explained to her the esteem in which cyclists were held in France, and how their very presence on the roads was enshrined in law, she began to come round.

"Apparently," he said, "if a car hits you it is always the driver's fault, no matter what."

Sensing that suggesting the possibility of being hit, had not been a good move, he quickly changed tack.

"They have to leave 1.5 metres between you and them when they overtake, and because of the liability bit they are super careful, or they're done for."

But then he ruined it again by using the Tour de France to illustrate how much the French revered cycling because Maisie's only recollection was TV footage of piles of cyclists spread across the road having just orchestrated a spectacular crash.

"Oh, I don't know Denis."

"And we can cycle to crêperies and things."

Ah. Bingo! Deal breaker!!

And that is what they were doing on this particularly mild sunny January day.

For Denis, the crêpe was a metaphor for the whole of French

cuisine.

"French cuisine! With its emphasis on flavour and presentation, simple chosen ingredients transformed, into something magnificent.! And the old crêpe, that classic Breton fare. With a little heat and a little time, flour, eggs and milk are converted into a delicious, filling meal. So noble, so magnificent in its simplicity." he extolled.

Er hmm, stay off the Pastis Denis.

Considering his apparent reverence of this Breton classic, Denis's reaction, when served with his chosen crêpe was always tinged with an immediate sense of disappointment? It all looked so minimal, like,

 "Where's the rest?"

But as he began to devour it, he was always seduced by the feeling that less is more, and that a crêpe is indeed, far greater than the sum of its parts, and so by the time he had consumed it, savouring every mouthful, he was always more than satisfied, fulfilled and filled full.

Of course, the overall taste did depend somewhat on the quality of its contents, and the skill of the chef. Denis had gone for the, *La Délice de la Mer* a stunning combination of: *'Noix de St Jaques, petits legumes crèmes* (celleri carottes courgettes).

Maisie, after a close encounter with some andouille somewhere in mid-France, was far less one for departing from things she knew, and her perception of a crêpe, being, like most people's, simply a pancake with stuff in it, had chosen a *'Complete'*, ham, egg and onions.

Simple, but very satisfying.

The pancakes had arrived like little parcels folded over at the edges and with Maisie's egg sitting proudly on the summit of hers, and Denis's constituents hidden inside, their little faces were alight with expectation. And they weren't disappointed.

"Mmm! Yumm!" Denis had uttered as he savoured the first mouthful of his scallops cooked in the creamy sauce.

"Mmm yum, yum!" he continued.

Maisie was equally taken with her choice, and for a while they sat silently appreciating their dishes.

Relaxing back into his chair and still relishing the lingering flavour of his chosen crêpe, he purred,

"Pass the dessert menu Maisie."

When in Brittany do as the Bretons do, had always been Denis's mantra, and so, though not normally a cider drinker, his crêpe was accompanied by a cidre brut, which was served in a classic terracotta jug and drunk from a similar little clay mug. It was equally delightful, and Denis was thoroughly enjoying the generous half litre of it until Maisie ruined it a little by asking,

"Are you aware of the drink cycling rules in France Denis?"

Choking ever so slightly on his latest quaff of cidre brut, his response was rather sheepish and somewhat vague.

"Er, um. Oh yeh, I never really thought of that Maisie."

"No, neither did I." she replied sipping on her Kia Royale.

"Just asking."

By the time that they had arrived at le Crêperie Le Lizen, Plouguerneau, they were ready for the refreshment it provided. Situated 14.8 kilometres west of Plouneour it hadn't seemed too big a challenge on paper but this was their first electric bike excursion of the trip, and though benefiting from having downloaded the directions onto their phones, they did not exactly know the way which meant quite a lot of stopping along the route to get their bearings. This had prompted a very uplifting encounter with a sweet old lady, who had enquired as to whether or not they were lost. Denis had to say, "Pardon madame" twice because he hadn't quite understood, though he reckoned that she was probably deaf. Which hadn't made any sense.

"Ah." he said. "She's asking if we are lost. Sweet."

The route was however remarkably flat, with only a couple of climbs along the way, which the electric bikes coped with admirably. Despite a few moments of concern for Denis that he may have set the bar a little too high for Maisie, he was comforted by the fact that they were heading for a crêperie, had their destination been a splendid view or an ancient Cathedral well, that would have been a different story.

"Can't be far now my little darling, you're doing ever so well."

Careful Denis. Maisie doesn't do patronising.

Maisie was leading the way and doing most of the navigation.

"Just keep the sea on our right." Denis had suggested trying to help. "Can't go wrong with that."

"Yes, that's great but where is the sea?" she shouted back.

"Good point." he thought. "We'll see it in a minute, it can't be far away."

"Really?"

"Right, here." she shouted

"Are you sure, it looks like a farm track."

"Right, here." replied Maisie ignoring him.

"Ok ok. Right here."

It was good to get off the main road, which although direct and not too busy, was busy enough, and noisy, so it had been a struggle to communicate, which had also caused quite a bit of stopping to check the route. Now off the beaten track, they were heading off down country lanes and Denis was beginning to think that the Crêperie Le Lizen might be more elusive than he had anticipated, but just as he was about to challenge his wife's navigation skills, not always a good idea, they rode around a corner, and there it was. It had taken them nearer to an hour and twenty minutes rather than the fifty minutes indicated on the route map, but it should be quicker going back.

"Blimey, it is quite hidden away, eh Maisie? I was imagining it being on the seafront at Plouguerneau."

But Maisie was already pulling off her helmet and heading inside.

After an initial bit of panic, when the owner after warmly greeting them, asked if they had a reservation, which turned out to be just an enquiry, they were soon seated in the lovely cosy room of the crêperie, and studying the menu. With its gingham tablecloths and roaring log fire, the ambience was just as Denis, ever the romantic had imagined it would be.

"Marvellous eh Maisie?"

And so, a little while later having tucked away the mains they were both now ready for dessert.

"Mmm I'm going for the *La Delice d'Antan* Denis. Ooer Crème de Marrons, caramel beurre, sale and chantilly. Yum!"

"Ugh, don't know how you can eat those chestnuts Maisie, they're far too sickly for me. I'm going for the *La Route du Rhum*, caramelized bananas, glacé rum raisin, caramel, Chantilly and amandes effilées."

"Sickly? Yes I see what you mean Denis."

There was silence at the table for the next ten minutes as they both ploughed their way through their respective French versions of diabetes on a plate.

"Café monsieur, madame?"

"Oh why not?" responded Denis

"Un café noire et un café grand s'il vous plait. Madame!" he said confidently.

As he sat glowing with satisfaction and listening to the hum of conversation he began to contemplate, never a good idea.

"Have you noticed Maisie?"

"Have I noticed what Denis?"

"Have you noticed? French conversation always sounds as if it is full of indignation."

"Denis!" responded Maisie furtively glancing around.

It had been a good day.

◆ ◆ ◆

Denis and Maisie wasted no time in exploring their new surroundings. Either by bike or on foot, as the weather had remained clement enough to accommodate either. Occasionally they might even take the car, usually to pick some supplies up from their nearest Lidl, or to explore further afield.

It had been the incident with the bottle of wine and the trolley token at the Lidl, which had led Denis to realise that he had actually progressed from his standard response when being taken by surprise by a stream of unexpected French. In the past, it had always been to immediately respond with,
"Er pardon, Je suis Anglais." whilst sporting an inane grin and beating a hasty retreat.

Their frequent stays with Jack and Symone in Pau had obviously progressed his command of the language a bit, though he had been disappointed that it wasn't as much as he had hoped. He had come to the conclusion therefore, that though he loved to learn new languages, and was always willing to try them out, he just wasn't very good at it.

However in the supermarket, he hadn't panicked at the young lady's stream of French, but carefully ran through her words in his head, managing to recognise enough, to piece together its meaning and therefore a sensible response, and it had worked. He still couldn't help the rather pathetic,

"Mais oui madame, mais oui." Along with the inane grin, but it had been progress.

Enough progress in fact, that a few days later whilst returning from a rather expensive moules frites, lunch in Roscoff, the cost of which may or may not have fuelled his response, though that also may have been the two very large glasses of Leffe. He had responded in a Supermarché to a classic example of French indignation, in a most un-Denis manner.

Not intending to buy very much, he had not bothered to get a large trolley with the little blue jeton, which the kind girl in Lidl had provided him with, and just picked up a little basket on wheels as he went in.

Of course, by the time he reached the checkout, he had accumulated rather more than anticipated, including six large bottles of eau de source (water, because the water in the cottage ruined his tea.) No problem thus far, until having placed his numerous items on the belt, and was just about to bring his trolley through to the other side of the checkout, he was stopped in his tracks by the cashier, abruptly announcing like some traffic policeman on steroids, that les trolleys were not allowed past this point, whilst indicating dramatically, where they had to be left. Had he been in any doubt as to what she meant, her loyal lieutenant, in the person of another indignant customer, was at the same time pointing dramatically at the same spot.

"Oh for goodness sake!" muttered Denis.

"Des réglés, eh, cuh." he added, trying to make light of it. But no, not funny Denis.

"Ah well." he thought, as he presented his card for payment, muttering to himself quietly about what he was supposed to do then.

Glancing towards the door he noticed some other odd-looking trolleys, very small, but big enough to get his purchases out to the car, where Maisie was waiting.

"Perfect." he thought, "Just the job."

Leaving his things at the end of the checkout, he went over and brought back one of the little trolleys. Well if indignation had accompanied his first faux-pas, it was nothing compared to the horror ignited by this transgression.

A veritable stream of gasps and shocked expressions were followed by a clear indication that this was strictly, 'verboten!'

Denis's reaction? No inane grins, no obsequious apologies, no, "Ah pardon madame." And definitely no, "Je suis Anglais" 's

Just Denis, resolved and seriously irritated. Having recently realised that the reason for him being so often put on the back foot, was because he did not understand, he let out his own stream in English.

"OK, so what the hell am I supposed to do with this lot then!!" he demanded in a far from quiet voice. "Yeh, pick the bones out of that!"

The response from the collection of customers now waiting at the checkout was a mixture of shock and embarrassment.

The response from the lady at the checkout, somewhat less officious now, was something along the lines of, well that's normal.

But Denis hadn't finished, oh no.

This time confidently in French, he followed up with,

"Oui, c'est normal Madame, mais il n'est pas raisonnable!!"

And with that, he proceeded to place his items on his little trolley and, fuelled with adrenalin, strode out of the supermarket doors and made his way to the car park.

"Where the hell have you been Denis, I thought you only went to get some bread?"

"Just had my first French bust-up Maisie" he replied. "Tell you about it when I get back."

"Denis!"

But Denis was on his way back with his trolley. The thought that there may be security waiting for him had never occurred, and anyway, he could not have cared less.

Maisie sat there, nervously waiting for the return, or not, of her husband and was extremely relieved when he did.

Her reaction on eventually hearing Denis's explanation was expected.

"Oh for goodness sake Denis, you're going to get yourself arrested!"

But secretly she was very proud of her little husband.

After they had enjoyed a couple of weeks in their own company, they were visited in Brittany by Clare and her latest beau.

Jacob or Jake, as he was introduced, was a rather strikingly avant-garde young man, certainly arty, who was very different to her usual choice of boyfriend and whom Denis, being Denis, immediately eyed with a little, well not suspicion but well, misgiving, yes that's the word. It was his long hair, his equally long flamboyant coat, and his general attire, which immediately caused Denis to feel a tremor of wariness, he was also rather overconfident for Denis's liking, and also rather fey. Maisie in contrast, was her usual welcoming self and, immediately recognising Denis's overprotective gene kicking in, wasted no time in letting Jacob know that he was a pleasure to meet, and not to worry about the grumpy old git, though the last bit, she didn't actually voice. They had already booked their by now favourite crêperie, and as they walked into Crêperie Le Lizen, Denis wasted no time in impressing Clare and Jake with his command of the French language, greeting the hostess as if they were old friends.

After studying the menu for a few minutes, Clare, indeed, suitably impressed with her Dad's command of the French language said,

"Jake's a vegan Dad. Can you ask the lady what is suitable for vegans?"

Clare looked earnest, Denis looked aghast, Maisie tried to conceal a smile, and Jake looked, well, fey.

"Gawden Bennet!" thought Denis.

"You're kidding!" he said when he had finally recovered some composure.

"I am not sure that they have vegans in France. What does it mean?"

"He doesn't eat meat, fish including shellfish, dairy products, or eggs." said Clare, helpfully.

"Or honey." added Jake.

"Honey?" enquired Maisie.

"No, commercial honey farming may harm the health of bees." informed Jake.

"Brilliant, bloody brilliant." Denis muttered as he made his way up to speak to Madame. "He's a bloody tree hugger!"

"Er, hmm, avez-vous, des nourriture pour vegans?" Denis said nervously to the lady, dismissively raising his eyebrows whilst at the same time gesturing in the direction of Jake.

"Yes of course." she replied in perfect English, "Not a problem Monsiuer." And went over to the table to discuss the various options with Jake.

It seemed that France was progressing rather more quickly than Denis. No real surprise there.

"Ah thanks Dad." said Clare.

"Yes well done Denis." added Maisie, smiling mischievously.

During the meal they had an interesting discussion about shellfish after Jake informed them that he was part of a group who were working towards more humane practices in the kitchen, which included banning the preparation of lobsters, crabs and other seafood, by plunging them live into boiling water.

Denis could only manage a muffled grunt as he continued to tuck into his Coquille Saint Jacques galette.

"It's only for a couple of days Denis. And he is a lovely boy." Maisie said, trying to reassure her husband that night as they lay in bed.

"Yes but he's not a man's man is he Maisie?"

"What the hell does that mean?" she replied. "Honestly Denis, sometimes!"

The next day, Denis and Maisie took them on a tour around the coastline, which wrapped around the whole area forming the huge broad peninsula, in which the village of Plouneour was situated. Though the day was quite chilly, the scenery was stunning, and they were soon strolling down onto the beach. Denis scrambled over some rocks to get a more panoramic view, whilst Jake collected various sea shells, which he planned to take home and use to make a mosaic for Clare.

Arm in arm, a little distance away, Maisie and Clare stood watching them.

"What do you think of him?" said Clare to her Mum.

"Oh he's lovely, he's a really lovely boy." replied Maisie reassuringly.

"I don't think Dad likes him." Clare continued.

"Oh come on, you know you're Dad by now, he just needs to get used to him, you know he's protective."

"I know but I wish that they could just become a little bit more friendly."

The cold bracing wind finally won over the draw of the impressive scenery, and they decided to find shelter and sustenance in a rather splendid-looking beachside hotel.

"See if they have any hot chocolate Denis." said Maisie settling herself down into a comfy armchair inside the hotel bar.

"Oh me too!" added Clare excitedly.

"Beer?" Denis called to Jake who was also already comfortably seated.

"Er, no thank you I only drink cider." responded Jake.

"Yeh, sounds about right." muttered Denis.

 "Bio if it's possible." Jake added.

"No it ain't." Denis replied to himself.

Er two hot chocolates, a draft beer, and a cider, please. Denis said in perfect French to the young man behind the bar.

"Oui monsieur. Er Grande?"

"What?" thought Denis slightly knocked off his stride.

"La bière? Oui." Denis responded grinning, "Mais oui!"

"Et le cidre?" Denis not used to such interrogation over a couple of drinks reverted to his default setting and said

"Ah oui, oui."

"Cidre grand?" the young man repeated.

"Er, oui" confirmed Denis with a little hesitation. "What's wrong with a big cider?" he thought.

The response of the young man, who looked about fifteen, seemed to suggest that he had not been employed for very long and perhaps never drawn a beer pression before, it was only after some faffing that he managed to draw Denis a large beer, that was dominated by a good two inches of froth on the top of the glass. In the meantime, Denis noticed that his beer was 7.8%!

"Oops better keep that quiet." thought Denis.

As someone who had grown up in the North of England, when he turned and noticed the rather significant shortage in his glass, he immediately pointed it out to the young man, who slightly bemused, nevertheless apologised and began to address it.

Denis trying to make light of it, then committed the cardinal sin of trying to make a joke in a foreign language, something Maisie was always reminding him not to do.

"Hmm, there are a couple of Euros worth missing there." he said laughingly.

"Deux euros?" the young man said even more puzzled.

"Nothing." said Denis, glancing across at his wife, who fortunately was too engrossed in conversation with Jake to notice, though she was beginning to wonder what was taking so long.

At that point, a comedy routine began to unfold, which would live in Denis's memory for years to come.

The young man tried to pour off the froth by attempting to tip the top of the glass down the sink, which resulted in most of the beer going with it. He then filled the glass up again, this time ending up with even more froth in the glass than before. For some reason, expecting a different result, he then repeated the same action, and again most of the beer followed the froth down the sink. After a couple of more goes, the increasingly flustered young man reverted to plan 'B'. Using a small wooden paddle, he proceeded to try to scrape the froth off the top, but the majority of the froth stubbornly refused to cooperate. Denis being unable to take any more, put the young man out of his misery, assuring him that it was fine.

When he finally got back to the table with his beer, he was exasperated.

"Why didn't he just fill the glass up till it poured over the top? He wasted more beer faffing around for goodness sake!"

"Calm down Denis, you're going to have a heart attack," said Maisie, "and anyway where's Jake's cider?"

"Oh bloody hell!"

Taking a large bottle of cider out of the fridge, the young barman showed it to Denis, who gave it his assent. He then, after opening it, proceeded to pour out a glass and put the rest of the bottle back into the fridge.

Bemused, but by now having lost most of his will to live, Denis delivered the glass to Jake who received it gratefully.

After a few slugs of his very nice 7.8% beer Denis was feeling much better, but after having checked his receipt, which included fourteen Euros for a bottle of cider, he still couldn't stop going on about it.

"Look." said Maisie, "He's just put it in the fridge to keep it cool Denis, that's what they do. Just ask for a refill when Jake is ready."

Denis did not waste much time finishing his drink, a fact not unnoticed by Maisie, and he went off to the toilet. When he came back another 7.8% bière grande was on the table.

"Oh thank you. That's very kind of you." he said to a smiling Jake.

"You're welcome."

Denis was warming to Clare's boyfriend.

"You ready for another cider?" Denis enquired.

By this time an older man had appeared at the bar, a very dapper and friendly chap, who called over effusively to greet his guests. He was obviously the boss and proceeded to both instruct and at the same time gently chide the young man as he took him through various procedures.

Denis took Jake's glass up to the bar and handed it over to the young man who was about to fill it with draft cider.

"No no!" Denis said, and explained as best he could, that they had bought a large bottle, and it was in the fridge. The young man even more confused than usual looked blank, but fortunately, at this point, the older man came to the rescue. Carefully explaining again that he had already purchased a bottle of cider, which was in the fridge, and showing him the receipt, the older gentleman whose English was about as good as Denis's French, i.e. not very, assured Denis that he understood, and filling two new glasses out of the bottle in the fridge, invited Denis to sit down before producing another new bottle of cider, which he opened and immediately brought over to the table, accompanied by the young man with the other two glasses of cider!

Realising that his guests were English, he then rehearsed with great enthusiasm just about every English word and phrase he knew, before skipping back to the bar with a big smile on his face. He then gently explained to the young man the nature of his mistake. He was a nice man.

Jake, faced with another bottle of strong Breton cider, thought better of saying that he had actually had enough, but invited Denis to help himself.

"Er, me and Clare will have an Irish coffee each." Maisie informed Denis, "It looks like we may be here a while longer."

Despite, or rather because of the little mix-up over the drinks, it was a very enjoyable visit and everyone was very happy. Well, after consuming two large 7.8% beers, and the best part of two large bottles of Breton cider between them, Denis and Jake certainly were.

Arms wrapped around each other like two long-lost brothers and singing Abba songs rather badly, Denis and Jake strolled off ahead of the girls.

"That what you meant by more friendly?" Maisie asked Clare.

"I don't believe it!" she replied. "I just don't believe it!"

After a couple of days, Clare and her boyfriend returned home. It had, after a shaky start, been a very enjoyable visit and Maisie and Denis would miss them. It seemed that Jake and Denis, with their slightly unconventional, albeit contrasting views of the world, had quite a bit more in common than had first appeared.

Regardless of Denis's late arrival at Jacob's vegan party, it didn't stop him from carrying out his intention of visiting the market in the nearby Brignogon, to buy a live spider crab, which with the assistance of a YouTube video, he proudly prepared himself. Though it was quite a laborious task, and the end result was a little sparse in terms of white meat, it made a delicious meal, and despite his wife's initial lukewarm response, she too enjoyed it.

Denis and Maisie continued on with their idyllic life in the little cottage for several more weeks, during which time they made friends with quite a few of the locals. One of whom, when he had told her about the spider crab, made Denis promise that he would put it into the fridge for an hour to sedate it, before he put it in the boiling water.

"Of course." he replied. "and should I put some little mittens on its claws?"

To which he received a rather puzzled look.

"Denis! Jokes!" said Maisie.

When not relaxing, they spent their days cycling and visiting several of Brittany's famous crêperies. They also had a couple of trips to Brest to a particularly good restaurant, where they had discovered delicious moules frites at a reasonable price.

One night on the phone to his son Jack, down in Jurancon, he was waxing lyrical about the wonderful way in which they had adjusted to life in France, and even treated him to a description of his culinary skills in his preparation of the spider crab, taking him through the whole process.

"Wow you're really becoming French Pops!" declared Jack's wife Symone. Jack was well impressed.

"Would you do it again Dad." he asked.

"Absolutely I would do the whole thing again! Oh yes from beginning to end the whole experience. No question I would!"

"Dad! Dad!"

"Yes, I would do it all again! I would do it all again I would, I would."

"Dad, Dad. DAD!!"…………...

FINALE

………."I would, yes I would…..."

"Dad! Dad! Are you OK?"

Within minutes Jack was there.

 "Just leave me a second Jack." said Denis, I've either broken something, or I'm OK. I remember it from football, I just need a few minutes."

As it turned out, Denis hadn't broken his knee, or anything else, and by means of carefully controlled sliding, using his outspread arms as breaks in the snow, he began to descend the slope. But by the time he had managed to negotiate his way down to the bottom, which at first, wasn't even visible, it was late and the day was done, as was Denis.

"I'm sorry dad, I'm so sorry."

"Don't worry Jack, you wouldn't believe where I've been…." his voice trailed off as he recalled the previous…five minutes.

Jack, worrying that his father was suffering from a concussion was impatient to get him home.

At least it had stopped snowing. An eerie calm had descended on the previously busy resort. Mind you it was nearly dark, the February sun having sunk below the snowy peaks ages ago. Having detached himself from his ski gear, Denis was beginning to feel a little more at ease. At least he was safe, and still in one piece, and he was already thinking of the Leffe beer and the steak, waiting for him back at base, but fate can be a fickle mistress, and it started with a troubling recollection.

"Did we tell your mother that we would pick up supper at the Super U on the way back Jack?"

Knowing full well that they had, though by now that seemed like several days ago.

"Yes, you did dad."

"Great! Bloody great!"

The journey back would be at least an hour and a half. They still had to get to the car, and then go shopping when they got back to Jurancon.

"ETA? At least, nine-thirtyish." Denis computed. "Maisie will be well pleased."

"Mind you, if they have been hitting the aperitifs at the usual speed, we might get away with it." he thought hopefully. "And anyway we're almost in Spain, they always eat really late there."

Good luck with that one Denis.

Jack was very quiet. He had noticed the change in the landscape after several hours of heavy snow. Although the main road through the village was pretty clear, the side roads, one of which lead from the car park, were quite difficult to see.

"Nine-thirty." he thought, "Hmm."

When they eventually found the car park his fears were

confirmed. The only way that they could identify their car amongst the wonderfully sculptured giant marshmallows, was that being a people carrier, it was a little bit higher than the others. The other vehicles all belonging to tourists who were here for several days, and already well into their après-ski, weren't going anywhere any time soon.

"You'd better phone your mother Jack."

◆ ◆ ◆

"Well I don't think that we should wait for them any longer, I'm starving." complained Gloria "It's nearly nine o'clock! You think they'd at least have phoned."

"Well Jack did try and get through an hour or so ago, but he just kept breaking up. All I got was, "D on't w o rry!!" offered Symone.

That was just what Maisie needed to hear. Mind you she was used to Denis's well-thought-out schemes going you know what up, and she had warned him. She was beginning to get ever so slightly agitated, but not necessarily due to concern.

Symone retrieved a large previously frozen bœuf-bourguignon from the freezer, and by the time it had been thawed out and heated up, the boys, having still not returned, were summarily abandoned, and it was soon polished off, mainly by Eddie and Gloria.

Maisie, due to a mixture of anxiety and anger, but mainly the latter didn't feel like eating. Symone, also used to her own husband's errant behaviour, never really worried about him, she knew that just like James Bond, he would complete the mission and get back to base eventually, maybe a little shaken, but never overly stirred.

Eddie's only concern was that he had finished off all of Denis's bottles of Leffe, still, it didn't prevent him from slurring a 'yes' to a third helping of the beef.

"I will kill him this time." said Maisie, ominously.

Meanwhile back on the other piste. Having finally identified the entrance to what was a car park earlier that day, fickle fate dealt them yet another blow.
"Brilliant! Don't you just love the random quirkiness." said Jack.

 "Mek sure thet yeu keep ze, 'IN' and 'OUT' of ze car park clear wiz your snow plough. Pierre."

The bit with the entrance and exit, snow-plough Pete had dutifully done, unfortunately his brief had not mentioned venturing into places like the parking bays, or even the area in front of the parked vehicles, which he had not done.

The mountain of snow secreting the Citroen Picasso had to be painstakingly cleared before the boys were going anywhere, and, if Denis who already felt like he had been hit by a truck, thought that he was exhausted before, by the time they had finished, he did seriously think that this time, he was going to die. It was only the enterprise of Jack, ripping down a sign saying, 'S'il vous plaît. Garer seulement dans les baies', to use as an improvised shovel, that made the task in any way doable.

 "Oh Lord, just watch a bloody gendarme pop his head up now." Jack thought as he shovelled away with the vandalised sign. But Denis was really past caring, he was no longer cold, just soaking wet.

◆ ◆ ◆

It was gone midnight when they arrived back, all thought

of eating a conventional supper abandoned long ago. Thank goodness Symone had overdone the packed lunch, long before they had reached home even damp rolls tasted good. Denis didn't wait for Jack to put the car away, he stumbled off down the corridor in a state of exhaustion.

Creeping quietly into bed, despite shivering uncontrollably, he felt a sense of achievement at having snuck in without disturbing the slumbering Maisie.

"Oh well." he thought as his sense of equilibrium slowly returned and fully appreciating the warmth of his dear wife's body.

"Maisie, you wouldn't believe where I've been today. It was really strange. Still," he continued,

"All's well that ends well, eh?"

That was until he heard the voice.

"Oh hi Denis. You're back then." said Symone, slightly awkwardly.

"Oh Gawd!!"

POST SCRIPT

"Bloody French!"

Cursed Denis as he managed, last moment, to swerve his unpretentious, B Twin, Original5, Grip Shift, leisure bike out of the way of some idiot's van door.

"Gawd-an Bennet, that was close!!"

It was only whilst replaying the incident later in his mind that he realised just how close his heroic swerve had come to redirecting him straight into the path of another vehicle coming up behind! Fortunately, that vehicle was a safe distance back and had had the time to slow down when its driver saw Denis's dramatic swerve, and more importantly, the reason for it. Instead of adding to Denis's 'injury' by insulting him with remonstrations about his sudden erratic movement, the driver actually slowed down and as he drove past, made animated thumbs-up gestures in the direction of our shaken hero whilst shouting,

"Bravo Monsieur! Bravo!"

Denis ruffled but otherwise still in one piece, continued on his pilgrimage to the nearest Lidl supermarket with a renewed sense of connection with his French cousins. He had been hailed as a hero by one, after being nearly wiped out by another, all in the space of a few moments.

"Bloody French! Don't you just love 'em!"

Rather appositely, it had been fairly recently that another one of Denis's romantic illusions about the French had been shattered. You know the one about their innate love of cyclists, and their desire to protect them at all costs being so strong, that they actually had it enshrined in law. Well it is, but as Denis had realised since becoming a member of the cycling fraternity, albeit to the shops and back, that if it wasn't spelt out in the law it wouldn't occur to many French drivers that wiping out the odd cyclist would be anything more than collateral damage and the roads of France would be littered with dead and dying cyclists.

His epiphany on this matter had been in the form of a very prim looking middle-aged lady who having sweetly waved him on at a crossing where he was patiently waiting to cross over with his bike, decided to go anyway because he hadn't reacted quickly enough. With exaggerated gestures of impatience and barely missing his front wheel, she revved off mouthing the French equivalent of,

"Snooze you lose, loser."

Denis's re-acquaintance with cycling had emerged as much out of necessity as for any other reason. He had come over to his beloved France in February for a short stay of six weeks. It was as a favour to their son Jack whose school were in desperate need of a 'supply teacher' of maths, to cover the back end of a maternity leave. His dear wife Maisie had joined him a few weeks later.

Denis was to complete the period of substitution which had actually been started by a very mild-mannered Indian guy whom the kids of years 7 and 8 had unfortunately eaten. Being, 'rough and tough and hard to bluff', Denis had, after much pleading by Jack, agreed. Well, he had asked himself,

"What the hell could go wrong in eight weeks?"

Ever practical Maisie responded immediately, "Actually Denis, plenty."

But even she had not anticipated what the 'plenty' would consist of.

Denis, who had not been to France since his little episode on the ski slopes, which still brought feelings of joy, pain and ultimate relief couldn't wait to set off.

"It's ski season." he announced, with no sense of irony.

 She had continued vainly, to inform Denis of the true length of eight weeks, if things didn't go according to plan. That he was well over 60 and that secondary kids don't, and never did, take prisoners.

Three weeks into his stint, just as Denis was beginning to bathe in the warmth of an, 'I told you so' moment, a global pandemic hit France. The whole place, shops, restaurants, bars, churches, streets, and complete towns, including schools, closed down. With air travel indefinitely cancelled Denis and Maisie were also indefinitely stranded and the parents of the teacher Denis was covering for could not fly over to look after her new offspring so she could not return to school. Almost poetry.

Now just entering his 18th week of online teaching Denis was on his way to do some essential shopping made only possible with the possession of Ministere de l'interieur form; *Declaration de Deplacement en Dehors de Son Domicile.* Which allowed escape from confinement for up to one hour and restricted the length of the journey to the closest supermarché.

For Denis 'Le confinement', as it was referred to, was not as bad as it might have been. As he constantly reminded his friend Eddie, who was presently similarly confined in the UK, being stranded in the South of France is a tough gig but somebody has to do it. In any case, though notoriously incapable of chilling for the sake of it, Denis's boredom was well and truly tempered by his online teaching commitment which occupied him for up to ten hours a day. Relaxing therefore was never really on the agenda. If you thought kids could be crazy in class try teaching them online! On one occasion, after painstakingly guiding the class through the wonders of 'probability'. One boy's response to the question as to what happened when a coin was tossed 50 times really took the 'bis, cuit'…..

"It fell off the table."

With a compact and bijou apartment, provided by the school, and a bicycle provided by Jack, if it hadn't been for the school work Denis would have been in his element. Two or three times a week, most days actually, he took himself off for a bit of hunter-gathering to collect the necessary provisions. A round trip of approximately 8 kilometres on an undemanding, flat, straight road with only a couple of French roundabouts to negotiate. It wasn't by any means the nearest shop but hey ho, who would ever know? Denis savoured the chance for some fresh air and the sight of the snow-covered peaks of the distant Pyrénees accompanying him all the way on his return journey literally capped it off.

One of the 'excursion' days would always be a Friday, the beginning of, 'le weekend'. Denis would rise early, set the work for the day and then take off to stock up on supplies to be back in time to receive the responses from his students. After a few more hours of checking, correcting and explaining, Denis and Maisie would settle down for a cosy evening of Netflix accompanied by a bottle of carefully chosen, 'Cote de Rhone Village' and some accompanying Roquefort or Cantal Jeune cheese, and sometimes even both! Some Fridays they would join Jack and his family and spend the weekend with them

Being a snug little 'garret', as Denis, ever the romantic called it, their accommodation afforded them little in terms of panoramic views nor outside space however it did have a view of the street below, and a large shuttered window which during the day allowed sunshine to flood in and later in the day the cool evening air.

Never one to be defeated by inconvenient surroundings, every day when the sun was at its zenith Maisie would stretch out a beach towel on the wooden floor of the apartment where the hot sun flooded in through the open shutters and lay there in her bathing suit. And, just like a chicken on the roadside rotisseries, turned over every so often making sure that she was evenly cooked.

The apartment was owned by Henri, an artisan boulangère, a very helpful and friendly chap who spoke as much English as Denis spoke French. Despite frequently interrupting each other's conversation with unintelligible French, or English, Denis and Henri immediately hit it off. Henri's little party piece had been to tell Denis and Maisie repeatedly that he was the fourth generation baker to run the business therefore, as he would say,

"You know, I am 'Enri ze fort."

"Very clever." thought Denis, who was desperate to explain the significance of Henry IV to Maisie but anticipating her apathy, resisted the urge, well, for as long as he could. Henri's often repeated line was always accompanied by exaggerated jolly laughter designed to convince the listener of the hilarity of the joke.

"How come he gets to make jokes in a foreign language?"

moaned Denis to himself. Still, he had long ago conceded that Maisie's 'advice' on the subject had been wise, as his own efforts had not always gone down too well. However, unable any longer to control his urge to inform, he satisfied himself by explaining to her that Henry IV had played a big part in the history of the area.

"Yes Henry IV who was King of France from 1589 to 1610 was actually born in Pau Maisie! That's why there are lots of references to him here in Pau Maisie, you know like the Château, Rue Henri IV, a Henri IV hotel, and others which I can't just recall. But yeh that's right, born in Pau eh? He was assassinated in Paris and was known as Good King Henri, again I can't quite remember why and….."

"Really Denis? That is fascinating."

In fact the flat, though not the Bohemian attic of legend, was situated directly above the bakery. And though this was obvious to Denis when he had first arrived, it wasn't until he woke up at 5 am on the very first morning that the ramifications became apparent. The original apartment had obviously taken up the whole first floor but had since been divided to provide the flat and accommodation for Henri and his wife. The dividing walls, therefore, were functional rather than practical and at five in the morning Henri's alarm went off and everybody, including Denis, woke up.

"Brilliant!" thought Denis. "A bloody nocturnal baker."

Unfortunately, it was about to get worse. Disturbed but unperturbed, Denis rolled over and quickly went back to sleep. He slept on for about a further hour until around 6 a.m. when Henri had managed to complete his first batch of chocolate croissants and the smell from them, though not unpleasant, began to seep through the floorboards and into Denis's nostrils.

It was to be a daily event that Denis, and latterly Maisie, had to get used to. Fortunately for Maisie, she always did manage to sleep through most disturbances and as for the smell of chocolate croissants, well she could learn to cope with that. For poor Denis 6 a.m. was it really. Despite the fact that he often did begin the day at the crack of dawn, a characteristic which often drove his wife to despair, this was usually in summer when they were camping and a whole day of adventure ahead of him, now in the depths of February there was only a day's teaching to look forward to.

Still, after the travails of the week, there was always Friday night treat night. Apart from the bouteille de vin rouge, or as Maisie preferred, G and T, the treat often consisted of duck breasts and chips. A culinary delight introduced to them by son Jack. Not quite so readily available in UK supermarkets, in this part of the world, the French appetite for magret de canard was up there with the ubiquitous moules frites and crème brûlée. Having been tutored by Gordon Ramsey via YouTube, Denis was quite the expert at preparing the tasty dish. He had even, as he saw it, discovered, that rather than wasting the rendered duck fat, he cooked the chips straight in it!

"Win, win!" Denis, as Denis often did, kept repeating.

"Oh yes," responded his dear wife, rather peevishly, "I am sure that you are the first one to think of that Denis."

The, 'once a week', treat night was as such for a couple of reasons. Denis having discovered that his weight had recently been creeping up north of fourteen stone had settled on a regime. A simple diet which consisted of not eating. It was the opposite of the well-known seafood diet, only this time see food but don't eat it. Taking advantage of the absence of her subversive friend Gloria, who found it difficult to resist temptation beyond a whole day, Maisie had joined him. So by Friday, after a week of work, work, work, in Denis's case anyway, very little food and no alcohol!! They were ready to embrace the weekend. The treat even extended to dessert. Often fresh juicy, ripe strawberries and crème-fresh (Mmmmm!) or sometimes, sometimes, a huge caramel, or chocolate pecan tart from Henri's bakery. (Oh stop, now I am struggling!!)

Some weeks, when Denis was feeling particularly flushed with the joys of living in his beloved France, the duck breasts treat extended to fillet steak instead. But before embarking on mission: 'filet de bouef' as Denis called this particular extravagance, he loved to research the different bouchères within cycling distance. After completing the necessary investigations, off he went on his bike to negotiate the deal.

On one particular occasion, he had been assisted in this task after bumping into Henri on the stairs. After the usual ritual of confusing each other with their own interpretation of the other's language, Denis on understanding the word 'superb', was clear that Henri was recommending a particularly good outlet at the Place de Foirail.

Denis knew that the amount of the French language that was required to accomplish the mission was limited and so by the time that he had done his 'prep' and finally strolled into the Charcuterie de Foirail in the Place de Foirail he, as on most occasions, felt upbeat and confident. Unfortunately, due in part to his obligatory and frequent rendez-vous with the law of sod, this was Denis's third attempt to get his fillet steak from this particular emporium. The first time it was closed until next Tuesday. The second time, on being relieved and excited to discover it open, he was immediately shattered on reading the sign on the door informing customers that the wearing of masks inside the shop was 'obligitoire' of course Maisie hadn't reminded him to take his.

"Oh gawd, bloody hell!"

But now at last he was here and after dutifully paying respect to the further notice on the door which forbade more than two customers in the shop at the same time, in he strolled.

Though mainly dedicated to a huge assortment of wonderful French charcuterie, including marinated duck breast, pates, various regional sausages, Terrine de Trois Rois, local rillettes, mousses, jambon de Bayonne from just down the road, and, the French equivalent of black pudding, the delicious boudin noir, the charcuterie also boasted an impressive choice of cuts of meat. Surrounded by these wonderful examples of French fare, Denis struggled to focus but there in the corner of the shop was the cabinet that contained his quarry. Clearly labelled, and looking sumptuously good and situated next to the entrecôte was, filet de bœuf.

Standing directly in front of the cabinet Denis began.

"Ah hem. Filet de bœuf, s'il vous plaît."

"Errh!!?"

Denis pointed at the rather large and totally conspicuous piece of beef fillet and tried again.

"Erm, filet...de...bœuf?? S'il vous plaît."

It suddenly dawned on Denis that he was once again encountering that charming French phenomenon,

'I am pretending that I haven't a clue what you are talking about mate because I am French and you aren't.'

A shrug, a look of total mystification and a further, "Errh??"

Denis adopted a different tack.

"Un kilo et demi de filet de bœuf s'il vous plaît."

"Ah, mais oui monsieur, filet de bœuf."

The sudden realisation regarding the purchasing intentions of the 'foreigner' by this particular boucher had well and truly evaporated any of his long-held grievances concerning, Agincourt, Crecy, Mers-el-Kebir or anywhere else. This truth was not lost on Denis.

"Actually, Mers-el-Kebir wasn't our fault." he mused, as Denis would.

"Un kilo et demi de filet de bœuf Monsieur. Bien sur!!" repeated le boucher, hardly managing to contain his excitement.

Denis realising that he had indeed finalised another deal in almost flawless French also felt a frisson of satisfaction. This lasted until Monsieur boucher, announced the price of his rather generous kilo and a half of fillet. Unfortunately, the clearly labelled fillet had not included a clearly labelled price.

"Ah oui, 60 euros." repeated Denis, attempting to sound casual.

"Merci Monsieur, merci." he continued, the colour rapidly draining from his face as he handed over his card.

"Merci a vous." le boucher replied with understandable zeal. "Merci a vous."

Clutching the heavy package under his arm Denis turned to leave.

"Au revoir." he said weakly as he left the shop.

"Au revoir, et bonne journée." Monsieur.

On his journey home, Denis's thoughts were dominated by how he was going to keep the finer details of this latest foray into French life from his ever-vigilant wife. He began to recall her gentle warnings the previous week when he had announced magnanimously to Jack,

"My treat Jack, my treat."

"You do know that fillet is expensive in the UK Denis," she had later warned.

"Goodness knows what it costs over here." she continued.

"I am sure that the kids would be happy with burgers, even if they are ridiculously expensive, but fillet steak!"

Happily for Denis Maisie did what Maisie often did. Later that evening as the filet de bœuf was unveiled in all its glory to shrieks of delight and, "Wow thanks Dad." Maisie contented herself with a look at Denis that said,

"I know, that you know, that I know, Denis!"

But Denis was still smarting anyway.

And so the fairly uneventful 'incarceration' continued without too much grief, as along with Maisie's improvised beach they managed to adapt to life with its variety of restrictions.

"There's worse things happen at sea." said Denis.

"Yes thought Maisie." recalling their little episode on the

Mediterranean of which Denis, it seemed, had apparently managed to expunge from his memory.

In fact, the biggest challenge for both Maisie and Denis continued to be the siting of the baking establishment directly underneath their bijou apartment.

Even though the realisation of this had impacted Denis's life on the very first morning of his stay, for Denis it was a mixed blessing. It did mean that he was never late for school, but being awoken even earlier than he was used to was a curse, though it was definitely emolliated by the gorgeous 'odeur'. Maisie, however, after initially welcoming the novel alarm clock, had latterly begun to struggle big time. It was like coming out of a dream, in which you are desperate to continue, into a nightmare of temptation. Despite the challenge, they did manage to resist with the odd exception. Sometimes on a Saturday morning, with no school commitments, Denis would sneak down to the shop and return to wake Maisie up with a cup of coffee and a variety of Henri's delights.

"That's why I love you Denis." she managed through a gob full of pastry.

Denis ever keen to embrace French life to the full had always been wanting to avail himself of the ubiquitous 'poulet roti'. And at a Sunday morning market just below the apartment in the square by the Hotel Gueuleton was a purveyor of just that. Sixteen euros did seem a bit steep but it must be good for that price he thought, he even spent another four euros on roast potatoes, about six of them in all. Observing from a distance, while Denis concluded the transaction, he could feel Maisie's scepticism burning a hole in his romanticism.

Well as it turned out it didn't taste a lot better than an ordinary supermarket chicken at which point the sixteen euro price tag started to register, but as he discovered later that day, it did act as a very effective laxative. Or was that the 14 euro (another vanity buy) bottle of red wine he had bought from a Specialist Wine Emporium. Or as they are called in England, an Off-Licence.

And so life continued fairly uneventfully. Well, oh yes apart from the confrontation with the gendarmes! Oh yeah, that one.

Just another routine day really, Denis up at the crack of dawn setting work online for his 40 year 7 and 8 students. Followed by his breakfast of Weetabix or at least a Lidl equivalent, before waking up the slumbering Maisie with a welcome cup of coffee.

It was approaching noon hour. After sorting out any little knots his students had managed to get themselves into regarding the work set, his thoughts turned to his daily bike ride to the supermarché, for essential provisions, wink, wink. But today due to a dodgy weather forecast Denis and Maisie had decided to do their permitted, *'l'activite physique individuelle'* a little bit earlier than usual. This little concession by the French authorities allowed the bearer of the appropriate paperwork to venture out of confinement within a radius of one kilometre of their residence for one hour each day for essential exercise.

Whilst on his 'jollies', Denis himself had never been challenged but had on one occasion witnessed a rather disturbing incident involving some unfortunate miscreant in a park. Regarding parks, and outdoor spaces, the rules were strict and clear with the clarity of the rules regarding parks being boosted by the fact that across the entrance to this particular one was a criss-cross of red and white tape with the words, 'Entrée Interdite' which would suggest to anybody with a pulse, French or not, that entrance to the park was not permitted. Anyway in a snapshot of life under pandemic restrictions, as he sped past on his bike, Denis viewed a young man, looking ever so slightly dishevelled having probably been caught on a bench in the park sleeping off the effects of his 'lunch', being clearly berated by a rather officious police lady who was making it very clear that the park though being in, 'normal' times, a public space was during ze lockdown, very much out of bounds. He was therefore breaking ze law! In desperation, the unfortunate young man, whilst pleading with her, was waving an equally dishevelled looking, *'Declaration de Displacement….',* Unfortunately, this did not cut the 'moutarde' with the zealous gendarme, who whilst, simultaneously raising the volume of her angry admonishment to the next level of hysteria, summarily snatched said, *'Declaration de Displacement'* etc. from his hand, ripped it up and threw it on the ground!

Witnessing the scene, however briefly, had slightly spoilt Denis's 'jolly' as he was reminded that stretching the spirit of the law, as he was doing, did carry some risks, he had seen what had happened to Papillion in 'Papillion' and he didn't fancy any of that. It was also at this point that the voice of Denis's own ever-practical admoniser began to echo in his ears.

"You will get caught one day Denis, mark my words!"

The incident having flashed by fairly quickly meant that Denis never got to witness the dénouement, and he was grateful because that also meant that he didn't get to see what the jovial police lady did next, but he was pretty sure that she wasn't about to offer to push the young man on the swings. Putting his head down, all Denis wanted to do was to get as much distance away from the angry policewoman and her colleague as possible. It certainly put the wind up him and it was several days before he ventured out again for his 'essentials'.

He hadn't told Maisie about it because although she wasn't really an, "I told you so." person she didn't need to be, he knew what her reaction would be. She had a knack for saying it without saying it and it messed with his head. Of course, Maisie knew as soon as he had arrived back that Denis had in some way had his fingers burned or at least his little cycling ass kicked. And even more annoyingly, once again, he knew that she knew that he knew too. Damn!

And so, by the time this day dawned, in Denis's head and for the time being, that particular event had naturally receded and remained only as a vague memory or perhaps at least, more accurately, a suppressed one. So as they set off carrying their necessary paperwork for their daily promenade, they left the safety of their compact and bijou apartment above, 'Le Pain Henri' without any sense of foreboding. The only variance to the early days of 'lockdown' was that things had progressed from a paper copy of the declaration to one downloaded onto a smartphone, this did turn out to be a significant difference. It was a particularly beautiful day and a stroll along le Boulevarde with its magnificent views of the Pyrénees beckoned irresistibly. Any indication of the arrival of the later rain was certainly not apparent.

Having, over the weeks, explored all possible routes and permutations of routes, they had a choice of two favoured ways. They would either go left across the road and straight down past the Gueuleton Hotel and straight up through a warren of charming little streets towards the Chateau before dropping down to the 'Boulevarde'. Or left and left again and along the narrow road past the Eglise Saint Jacques and then right up to the precinct and along to the Place Georges Clemenceau. On the far side of the square, the road wound around to the other end of the Boulevarde from the alternative route. Either way arrival at this famous Pau feature afforded a spectacular panorama across the valley of the Gan River to the Pyrénees, which from this viewpoint, seemed in touching distance.

Ever conscious of the one-hour limit, Denis after a length of time, took out his phone to check whether they should be heading back.

"Oh gawd Maisie, it's gone!"

"What's gone Denis?"

"The thing, the bloody paper thing, the permission!"

"How did you manage that, Denis? We did it at the same time."

"It looks like I downloaded it but never saved it to the phone."

Denis's voice rose in panic as he began to feel ever so slightly naked.

"Oh for goodness sake Denis! How long have we been doing this?"

"We'd better head back the way we came straight away." said Denis.

Maisie not enjoying the same benefits of regular fresh air afforded to Denis by the addition of his regular shopping outings, responded in a rather, un-Maisie, fashion.

"Oh come on Denis we are over halfway round. We have never ever seen a gendarme on any of our dozens of daily strolls. Look we'll carry on around to the boulevard and back around that way. It's no further."

Delivered by Maisie in a way that it was obviously not intended as a suggestion, Denis, after a very brief and pathetic effort to argue, capitulated.

Unfortunately, as they rounded the road leading onto the

completely deserted boulevard, Denis's fears, which had prompted his rare sensible response, were realised. In the distance looking straight back at them, Denis and Maisie sighted a checkpoint with two gendarmes and a police van. As the blood drained from Denis's face all he could see was the angry officious police lady at the park entrance ripping into her dishevelled victim. They had a decision to make. They were a long way from the checkpoint so they could turn around and head back the other way but they had been clocked by the officers. So in actual fact, they didn't really have a decision to make.

Maisie strolled forward resolutely, well she might, after all it was Denis who was going to Devil's Island. Denis went through his litany of the Saints pleading with each one to intervene, he was however slightly buoyed up by his wife's apparent coolness. Poor lamb, it hadn't occurred to him that it was only him that didn't have the correct paperwork.

"Don't say anything Denis."

Despite the heat, the helmeted law enforcers were dressed all in heavy black uniforms, and burdened with an array of accessories, truncheons, radios, pepper spray, guns and handcuffs and looked more like commandos than local 'bobbies' and they were certainly not in the mood to act as tourist guides. But in any case, Denis by this time had entered into a state of gay abandon. Unable to see how they were ever going to get out of this, he had simply drifted into what could only be described as, 'an out-of-body state', where he wasn't actually there and was allowing things to unfold as they would while he merely looked on clinging to the belief that, 'The Lord will provide.' Maisie, as ever, was slightly more practical.

Stepping forward purposely, she said confidently, "Bonjour Monsieur."

"Bonjour Madame." came the reply.

And then something along the lines of, 'show us your thingy.'

Maisie immediately produced her phone and, as if she had just whipped out a small revolver, was immediately told to,

"Step back!"

Now, this is where the fact that the French authorities had not really thought this through, began to come to the rescue. The screen on the phone was small, the pertinent document long and typically wordy and the sun high above the mountains was behind the officer and, like a shade-less lightbulb in an interrogation cell, was glaring onto Maisie and the phone in her hand. This was compounded by the demand that Maisie should keep her distance which meant that every time she ventured forward to afford the officer a better view, the subject of interrogation was greeted with an angry,

"Arrêtez!!"

Of course, this 'arrangement' didn't help the policeman's efforts to check for correct paperwork and the slight flaw in ze law, was not lost on Denis who having spotted a possible escape route, began to emerge from his trance. Though he didn't have his paperwork, he did have his passport, the carrying of which was another requirement in order to venture outside. Risking the possibility of being blown away by a Spectre M4 handgun, Denis whipped out his passport and waved it in the face of the other policeman.

"Passport, passport." he declared with his face a picture of innocence.

Rather than welcoming Denis's attempt to speed up proceedings the young officer barked.

"Get back! Get back!"

Denis duly did.

The other exasperated policeman, still vainly trying to read Maisie's document, was further frustrated by the kerfuffle caused by Denis. What had begun as a seemingly appealing opportunity for the two young law enforcers, to flex some authoritative muscles, was quickly descending into a bit of a French farce. Finally having motioned to Maisie to manoeuvre herself slightly clockwise, Gendarme Antoin was able to confirm that she was indeed in possession of the correct paperwork. Now, he thought what about her simpering companion? But by this time, and seeing Denis's best impression of being pathetic, Antoin had had enough.

"Oh mon Dieu, allez allez." he managed to command.

Not waiting for a second invitation Denis and Maisie quickly began to depart the scene, obsequiously thanking their interrogators as they went. But before they had managed to get too far Antoin's companion shouted something which sounded ominous.

"What he say? What he say?" demanded Maisie as quietly as she could.

"Go straight home." replied Denis.

Having had their authority somewhat compromised, the Gendarmes felt that the final command, to go straight home, had at least put them back in control, well slightly. Maisie and Denis, without looking back, just gave a compliant wave and didn't stop until they got there. On that particular day, their

Friday night treat was brought forward and yes, they did sleep very well that night.

◆ ◆ ◆

Whilst the compact and bijou residence was perfectly adequate for their needs, prior to Maisie joining him, Denis had been a little concerned that it might not match up to the picture of their little apartment in the South of France that he was sure she would have created in her mind so he had tried to temper her expectations without going over the top. However, his ever practical wife immediately saw the potential of their rather spartan dwelling and, shortly after her arrival, it received the benefits of Maisie's female touch. Aided by the purchase of a couple of items from a local brocante, including a simple wrought iron side lamp, the rather spartan accommodation had been transformed and was now, rather cosy. There was one thing though. It turned out that Henri's pain au chocolates weren't the only thing that would keep them awake.

On his arrival back in February, Denis had soon settled in both to his teaching and to his lodgings. In fact, having departed in a bit of a hurry, the previous resident, of Asian origin, had left behind quite an assortment of provisions which, apart from a year's supply of washing powder, included all the necessary ingredients for several authentic curries, complete with a freezer load of chicken! After a couple of nights, Denis had also got used to his new bed which though comfortable would perhaps be a little on the small side when sharing with Maisie, but that was for another day or night. And apart from the odd snore from his landlord which occasionally permeated the walls, which when he first heard it seriously freaked him out (true story), by Wednesday of his first week, he was retiring early, around 9pm and enjoying the sleep of the just. However, Thursday was not a good day at school. Denis had had to illustrate to a particularly annoying Spanish student that he had not just come down on the last raindrop but if he wanted to continue being a burro's ass then he was welcome to, 'bring it on'.

Denis therefore, had arrived home that day, tired and ready for his bed. After eating and prepping for the next day's teaching, he was soon blissfully in the land Zzzz's. That was until shortly after 9.30 when he was awoken by a hideous scream from the bar in the side street, right opposite his bedroom window. With a few tables on the pavement the curiously named, 'Au Fut et a Mesure' seemed to attract only a few visitors every evening and by the time it was Denis's bedtime most of the punters had drifted off and all was quiet. Generally, the glow from the lights provided a warm ambience in his bedroom and before closing time, the gentle hum of quiet conversation had provided Denis with a sense of company. Unfortunately, the scream which woke him up on this Thursday night was repeated at regular intervals over a rather long period of time as the woman who owned it broke into a regular cackle of manic laughter.

"Oh gawd. Maisie'll love this. And I'm working tomorrow! TGIF" thought Denis as he tried desperately to conquer the disturbance and return to sleep.

Goodness knows at what time the racket abated but the next morning Denis awoke to feel less than chilled.

"Thank God it's Friday."

Unfortunately, the Thursday night disturbance proved not to be a 'one-off', but merely a prelude to the weekend. Friday was worse and on Saturday nights it sounded like a veritable Mardi Gras was parading through the bar opposite. Going forward things were not looking good for Denis and Maisie in the sleep department.

However, things are never as bad as they appear. The inevitable total lockdown, precipitated by the onset of the pandemic, had included the, 'Au Fut et a Mesure', every cloud.... So calm was once again restored, at least until May when restrictions began to be lifted. A combination of the lengthening days and rise in evening temperatures resulted in the bar growing in popularity and the late-night revelry of the weekends returned and in fact, increased.

On the plus side, Denis and Maisie would often spend the weekend with Jack and his family in their quiet suburb and by Sunday night things had subsided once again to a reasonable level of normality. This happy arrangement of the weekend retreat was compromised a little with the continuation of the confusing ruling, which meant that mixing with others outside the household bubble was still strictly forbidden. However, with its distinct lack of clarity, added to the tendency of the egalitarian French to dismiss many of the thousands of rules and regs imposed upon them with a Gallic shrug; the Wilson 'family bubble' proved, as bubbles by nature are, flexibubble.

However, by the end of May, things were heating up and without the benefit of air-con, the compact apartment was beginning to heat up with it. By now weekend nights often involved the dilemma of having the shutters closed and trying to sleep in a sauna or with the shutters open, trying to sleep through the local carnival! Denis and Maisie were ready for home. They had already had a flight from Toulouse to Bristol cancelled, last minute, at the beginning of May and in any case, neither could the cavalry, in the persons of the parental baby minders, fly-in.

Denis's anxiousness to get home was further stimulated by his need for a dentist. Shortly after his arrival and during total lockdown, he had mysteriously broken a perfectly healthy front tooth whilst eating a piece of soft baguette with, cream cheese on it!

"Bloody hell! I've snapped me bloody tooth!" he cried.

"Yes I know, I heard it crack from over here." responded Maisie helpfully, as she glanced over from her magazine.

Jack had managed to secure him an appointment with an emergency dentist who had patched him up but only temporarily and that had been nearly three months ago.

But by the end of May they were spirits were rising, they were as confident as they could be, that a rearranged flight in early June would finally repatriate them and it was Denis's birthday.

It was a glorious day and they decided to go for a picnic. By now restrictions on movement had been relaxed markedly so they were not so anxious about bumping into their friends from the local Gendarmerie and decided to head for a park situated way below the Boulevarde on the banks of the River Gan. They took with them a whole host of salamis and other cooked meats, cheeses and of course some treats from Henri's bakery, including his irresistible caramelised pecan tart. Drool! They needed some liquid to wash it down which they picked up on the way at the local Monoprix. As they couldn't agree on red or white they opted for one of each, but of course, they wouldn't drink all of it, my goodness no, after all, it was only midday. Spreading out their indulgent picnic onto a large red blanket, which Maisie had borrowed from the apartment, they settled down to enjoy the afternoon. Unfortunately, the balmy weather had brought out a host of marauding mosquitoes which Denis had not really noticed until several of them had helped themselves to a bit of him.

"Oh bloody hell, I've been bitten!" he moaned.

"Just come and sit next to me, and I'll be fine." his dear wife instructed sympathetically.

Still, Denis thought, it wasn't going to ruin his day. But as he tucked into another mouthful of duck pate and a quaff of Madiran, his phone beeped.
"Oh bloody merde, oh flippin merde. The flight's been cancelled again!"

The news kind of put a damper on things as without the same enthusiasm they continued to plough through their various delights, not saying very much, what was there to say. Denis being a glass half full rather than a glass half empty person, reflected that here they were on a beautiful day, his birthday, in a beautiful park in France having a lovely picnic, come on it's not that bad. Maisie was less philosophical and, despite their resolve, as the food began to empty so too did the bottles until eventually, they were empty.

They must have cut a pretty sight, stretched out on the grass fast asleep and surrounded by the remains of a veritable feast and more significantly two empty wine bottles.

Ooh la la, les Brits, what are they like?

Incarcerated for the foreseeable and after discovering a, 'closing down sale' in a local art supplies shop, Maisie busied herself painting pictures which, by the time they left the apartment, had filled most of the wall space in it and most of Jack's house too! Denis's workload did not diminish with time though his, 'active' pupils did, many of them were citing 'technical issues' as excuses for not completing work but conscientious Denis still felt he had to chase them up. He did for a while join in the impromptu evening sing-along across the apartments of the narrow streets which he was enjoying immensely. He even borrowed a guitar from Jack to do some solos.

"Brilliant." thought Denis, "So French."

However he had to stop on Maisie's advice when he began to attract the attention of some local, ne'er do wells, who started to gather and shout,

"Hey rost beef, play us a song!"

Which was OK until it soon began to descend into some colourful abuse.

Despite the restrictions they did manage, under the cloak of darkness, to pay discrete 'family' visits to Jack and the rapidly growing Sophie. They even managed an undercover children's party at the house of one of Jack's friends where Jack managed to impress his friends' kids with a flawless attempt at apple bobbing, though it did leave himself and the whole floor, soaking wet.

The children, four of them, all very sporty, competitive and ridiculously good-looking, were not easy to impress. The eldest Jonty, as a lover of all things done in water, admired the way in which Jack had been willing to nearly drown himself to achieve his goal. Linus, or 'hot shot' as he was better know among his peers, of whom he had few, and who couldn't decide whether he would grow up to be Neymar or Mbape seemed a little disappointed that Jack hadn't actually drowned. The inseparable twins, Yvonne and Norman who excelled in any sport in which they participated were just gob-smacked that an adult could be so entertaining!

The climax to the evening of fun and laughter came when prompted by her proud parents, one of the neighbours' children, Eve, who knew all the songs from the musical 'Madagascar' sang and danced her way through the whole lot! Despite the looks on the faces of Jonty and Linus, the round of applause at the conclusion was fulsome.

So Denis ended up completing the school year. His original brief, "It's only six weeks Dad." turned out to be closer to six months. But still, where would you be rather locked up for six months Plymouth or the South of France? Even Maisie didn't have an answer to that one.

Henri the fourth was sad to see them go but appreciative of the lamp and the veritable art collection that they had to leave behind. And they were sad to leave, as Denis called it, their little French 'love-nest', steady Denis, that had been their home for nearly half a year.

They eventually procured a Ryanair flight to Stansted at the beginning of July, where Clare drove to pick them up. After praying desperately to get home for the last several weeks the flight took off from Lourdes!

Given the circumstances, it was with some relief, certainly to Maisie, that they were safely back home.

"But when will we ever be able to return to the green fields of La Belle France." Denis reflected.

PETER HANRAHAN

Well, now you know!!!!!!

Printed in Great Britain
by Amazon